"Sara Walker is an author to watch!"

-- Eve Silver
national best-selling and award-winning author of The Game
trilogy from Katherine Tegen Books.

Catching A Sorcerer

Sara C. Walker

*****

Melantha Caldwell series
CATCHING A SORCERER
HUNTING A DEMON
SAVING A SPELL TURNER - coming soon
Sign up for my newsletter so I can let you know as soon as it's available: *http://eepurl.com/Wi3mL*

CHAPTER ONE

SUNDAY NIGHT AND I was learning to turn a summoning spell. Though I'd spent most of my life being home schooled, I had a feeling this was not a normal family activity for other fifteen year old girls.

"Gran, when I told you I wanted a cell phone, this wasn't what I had in mind," I said.

Gran picked through a handful of wheatberries, looking for just the right one to add to her pot. We stood at opposites sides of the round table with a copper pot in front of each of us and a host of ingredients filling the table between.

"Cell phones don't work for members of the magical community," she said.

"What community? It's just you and me."

Dumping ingredients into a pot had nothing on the convenience of electronic communication. Kids at school were constantly using theirs to call each other, text, watch videos. But not me. I wasn't allowed to have one. I had to learn the "old ways."

Gran sighed, and I knew by the way her lips were pursed that she didn't intend to elaborate. She'd been trying to get me to learn spells every night for weeks now. I'd finally caved in hopes she would back off, but that plan hadn't worked out quite like I'd hoped.

"I have to go to the library tonight," I said. I dumped a handful of crispy dried lavender flowers—for devotion so the line of communication would stay clear— into my pot.

In another time we might have been called witches. But now that term was considered derogatory. We were spell-turners. Well, Gran was. I wouldn't be a full spell-turner until I turned sixteen and came into my full powers. In all my fifteen years, in all the time I'd spent in Halifax and my current residence in Ottawa, I'd never met another turner, not another magical creature of any kind, until the day my mother died.

If there was a magical community out there, I wouldn't know it.

I hadn't been out of the apartment except to go to school in six weeks. I needed to get away, to hang with some friends— even just for a little while.

"We have books here," Gran replied in a stern tone. This was an old argument.

She was right— we had books here. Every wall of the living room was filled to the ceiling with shelves, every shelf filled with books. All had belonged to my mother.

Without coming right out to say so, Gran was subtly reminding me of the reason I was confined to the apartment. My mother had been killed by a black-spell sorcerer— that is, a sorcerer who chooses to use death to fortify his spells. For some reason Gran thought he would come after me. But I wasn't a full turner yet. I had only partial powers. Until my sixteenth birthday, every spell I turned would dissipate the moment it came together. "Learning powers," Gran called them. "Just enough juice to see what you're doing, but not so much as to harm yourself or anyone else."

She seemed convinced I had these learning powers, but for some reason my spells never seemed to turn out right no matter how carefully I followed her instructions. And that was bad news. Even though they didn't want me to know, I'd heard my mother and Gran fighting about me. Gran thought I was either a late blooming white turner or a null— a turner's daughter born without powers. My mother refused to believe I was a null. So Gran was on a mission to prove one way or another I had learning powers or I was deliberately faking not having them out of extreme laziness.

"Your mother was a good white turner," Gran said. "She loved turning spells with me when she was your age. Couldn't get enough of it."

Her mention of my mother hit me square in the gut.

"Didn't she like to do anything else? Anything normal?"

Gran pinched her lips together again. She didn't like to speak about my mother beyond her gifted spelling abilities.

I directed the conversation back to the topic at hand.

"I really need the books at the library," I said. I followed her actions and, using a wooden spoon, swirled in two cups of diluted bay leaf extract for strength. I turned the spell clockwise, same as she did. We were on opposite sides of the small round kitchen table, so I had to think for a minute which way to turn my spoon.

"Why?" Gran asked suspiciously, narrowing her eyes. Everything was suspicious to Gran.

I barely kept myself from rolling my eyes. "I have homework."

"What homework?"

"What do you mean? I go to high school now. I get homework." I used to be home-schooled. Right up until 52 days ago when I lost my mother. Then Gran had to take over as my teacher. She used to be able to teach my lessons for the few months of the year when I went to live with her in Halifax, but now that I was in grade ten, my studies had advanced to the point where she didn't understand anything in my textbooks. So she marched me down to the nearest high school. She would have signed me up right then, but they were closed for winter holidays. Imagine that.

"The new semester starts tomorrow, February second, according to the literature I received from the school," she pointed out.

Crap. "I'm catching up from last semester," I said, carefully examining a handful of calendula. I felt more than saw Gran carefully examining me.

"Who's the boy?" she asked.

"There's no boy," I answered quickly. Too quickly. Double crap.

"I might not know much about quadriplegic equations or—"

"Quadratic equations," I corrected.

"Or, what goes into a good Theseus statement, but—"

"Thesis statement. Theseus killed the Minotaur."

"But," she said again with emphasis, ignoring my corrections, "I know my granddaughter."

This time I did roll my eyes. "Whatever."

His name was Rory Macdonald. But I wasn't about to tell Gran that. I met him in the principal's office on the morning of my first day. It was his first day, too. A drunk driver had killed his parents and now he was living with his aunt. I met him again later in the day at the guidance counsellor's office. A special grief counsellor had been brought in to meet with us. Neither of us wanted to meet with her, but nobody asked us. His aunt was almost as controlling as my Gran.

We didn't have plans for tonight, so I didn't have to worry about calling him to cancel. He'd mentioned he'd found this place, where he liked to go on Sunday nights to play bass guitar for a band. I'd only hoped to stop in and hear him play.

"You may invite him to come here," Gran said, ignoring my denials.

She released three drops of cedar oil, for dedication, into the liquid swirls in her pot. "But you won't be going out."

I bit back a scream. It used to be my mother and Gran had no trouble keeping friends out of my life, what with shipping me off to Halifax twice a year and homeschooling me. I never got to go to birthday parties, Halloween parties, camping trips or any other fun thing that normal girls did.

"Friendship is dangerous," Gran would say. My mother would agree. She would even agree when they were having that big fight that lasted for weeks.

I tried a new angle. "I need to use the computers at the library."

"What do you need those confounded contraptions for?" she asked. Her tone was one of surprise, even though this wasn't the first time we'd talked about my needing a computer for schoolwork. She just didn't get the concept of computers. Ever.

I listed the reasons on my fingers. "Research, report presentation, statistical analysis—"

"Hmph. In my day we had to do all of that by hand." She peered down her nose at the runny swirls in my pot. While mine was little more than a pathetic soup stock, hers had taken on shimmering hues of purple and green. I didn't have to see her face to know she was disappointed.

Still, I pressed my case. "Look, it's not a big deal. I can take care of myself."

"Hmph." She tapped the wooden spoon on the pot rim.

"Please? Can I go for an hour?" Oh, man. That sounded so desperate.

"No," she said simply, placing her spoon on the table next to her pot. She carried the empty vials to the sink and turned on the hot water.

"Gran—" I cried.

"I cannot permit it, Melantha. If you do not go outside this apartment with me, then you do not go outside this apartment at all."

I rolled my eyes and groaned. "You are completely impossible!"

If my words stung even the slightest, she didn't show it. She carried on with washing the dishes. "I'm sorry, Melantha. But I promised your mother."

"Promised her what? Promised you would keep me a prisoner and never talk about her?"

I slumped into a chair with my arms crossed. This was hopeless. Gran was super stubborn. I needed a new approach.

Temporarily abandoning my potion, I snagged the tea towel on the way to the sink. Unexpected helpfulness always put Gran in a good mood. I hoped it would be good enough to let me out.

She cleared her throat. "Your potion is incomplete."

"My potion is nothing but water with twigs and leaves in it." I noticed she didn't tell me not to dry the dishes. Nor did she tell me to start over and make the potion again. We'd been down that road before. It always resulted in the same thing: failure. Whatever it took to make a potion, I didn't have it. My mother and Gran had been convinced my spells would come together the closer I got to my sixteenth birthday, but so far they always amounted to nothing.

"Did you project your light into it?" she asked in that snippy tone that said she already knew the answer.

"Yes." I hated it when she said "light" instead of "magic".

"And?" Gran prompted.

"And what? Nothing happened." I shrugged. I felt my power, my magic. It flowed through me, the same as blood and oxygen flowed through me. It was there. I could feel it the entire time we put together these spells. But magic also dredged up too many memories of my mother. And there wasn't much light there when I thought about how she died. It was more like a choking sensation. I hated that feeling.

"You're not trying hard enough," Gran said. That was what she always said. I didn't answer. There was no point. She'd already made up her mind.

Maybe the truth was, I could have tried harder, but turning spells just felt wrong. If my mother had been killed by bullets, would I still be expected to attend target practice?

"I don't understand what's so bad about having friends," I said, plucking a soapy plate from the drain board.

She shut off the water. "You know the reason. They can be used against you. And you against them. It's better for everyone if you just don't have them to begin with."

Yeah, I'd heard that part before. It was stupid. For some reason my mother and Gran thought I would be kidnapped and held for ransom. I couldn't understand why. We didn't have anything of value. It wasn't like we were millionaires.

So who were they protecting me from?

"As for going out alone," Gran continued as she washed a pot, "there are many kinds of evil out there. You are not safe on your own."

"But I won't be on my own. I'll be with friends!"

"Together you'll be on your own."

"But that makes no sense at all!"

An eerie wind howled outside the windows. If the weather was getting worse, I was sure to lose this argument. I crossed the apartment to the living room windows and used the tea towel to clear away the condensation on the cold glass. Snowflakes swirled under the streetlights below. Even the weather wanted to keep me inside.

There was a sharp knock at the door. I met Gran's gaze. She appeared as surprised as I was, but where I welcomed any and every visitor, I knew she would send away whoever was on the other side of that door. By the expression on her face, she suspected I'd invited a friend over without permission. I hadn't, but knowing Gran, that wouldn't make a difference.

I dove for the door, but Gran beat me to it. She leaned cautiously up to the peephole.

"Open up, Alberta. I'm here to speak to the girl." It was a man's voice — muffled, old and tired. The voice of someone older than Gran, someone ancient.

The girl? I hoped for his sake, he wasn't referring to me. There was something familiar about the voice, something that sent a nervous sense of foreboding all the way down to my toes. This was one visitor I didn't want to see.

CHAPTER TWO

I WAITED FOR Gran to check with me, to ask if I knew this person, or to seek my approval for letting him in, but to my surprise she didn't do any of that. She just opened the door and invited him in.

I knew it was trouble right away. Only Council members carried those shiny black walking canes. No one else could even touch them. It was the cane I saw first, and the elf carrying it second.

Elves were an ancient race. They had very few magical abilities, there were even fewer of them on the planet, and virtually all of them served on the Council. This was the second time I'd met this particular elf. The first was in the hours after my mother's death.

It was the Council's job to investigate illegal use of magic. They were supposed to be investigating my mother's "untimely demise" as they so ambivalently put it.

It seemed someone on Council didn't believe my mother was murdered by magic. Someone said she took her own life. But I knew my mother. She would never do that. She would never choose to leave me.

If the elf was here to speak to me, then perhaps he had an answer.

In that moment, my chest tightened. Blood rushed in my ears, sounding like waves on the ocean. Magic or suicide. What difference did it make? Neither answer would bring my mother back.

I was marching toward my room when he called out, "Melantha, come here a moment, won't you?"

There was humour in his voice. A patronizing humour. And it pissed me off as much as the reason for his glee: I'd gotten as far as three steps and then slammed into some kind of invisible barrier. It was a soft, unseen shield that moved like Gran's cranberry jelly and repelled me the same way two alike poles on magnets pushed against each other. The harder I tried to force my way through, the stronger it pushed me away — until I got so mad and threw myself at it only to land hard on the floor. And the elf merely laughed.

Dusting myself off, I turned around and glared at him. He tapped his cane on the floor. "Come and sit a spell." He cackled at his own pun.

Fashion sense was not among the few powers possessed by an elf. He wore a powder blue shirt under a royal blue suit complete with a matching top hat, which he'd removed when he entered and now held in his hand. He seemed grandfatherly with pale wrinkled skin, cheeks stained bright pink from the cold. He had small eyes and ears that were pointed at the tips, characteristic of all elves. Or so I'd been told.

His formal wear was a strong contrast to Gran's hand-knitted fuchsia cardigan over gray track pants and a once-white t-shirt. She ran a hand through her short, white curls. I don't know if she was attempting to fluff them up or smooth them out. The end result was no different from when she started.

"Whatever you came here to tell me, you can tell it to Gran," I said, crossing my arms over my chest. I didn't dare turn my back to him or try to leave again. It wouldn't have gone over well, and with something as old and powerful as an elf, I didn't want to risk making him angry. He may have few abilities, but the ones he had were powerful, concentrated.

He sighed. "I'd forgotten how stubborn and ignorant teenagers can be."

"Ethelwulf! She is a grieving child, and well-entitled to her feelings no matter what they be at this time. Name calling is inappropriate!"

"You wish to contest that Melantha is stubborn? Or are you suggesting she is an expert in etiquette and therefore wasn't storming from the room a grandiose childish gesture?" He actually had the nerve to wink at me.

Gran fixed him with a look. The kind of look that usually had me running for the cover of my bedroom.

But not this elf.

He sighed again. "You're right, Alberta. I do apologize. I don't get out into the human world often," he said. "Nevertheless, she does need to hear this."

"You know who— who hurt my Lavinia?" Her voice timid and quiet, and very un-Gran like.

I stiffened. It was the first time Gran had used my mother's name since that awful night two months ago. I'd only heard "your mother" since.

He nodded. "We know."

I felt like my insides had softened and fell away like Jell-o sliding off a plate. He knew who killed my mother. I slid down and sat beside Gran on the couch.

"Then justice will be served." Gran gave a nod. She sniffed and the elf pulled a handkerchief from his pocket. She used it to wipe her eyes and nose.

"It's not as simple as that," he said softly. "I'm sorry."

"What do you mean?" I protested, staring at the elf, willing him to tell me it wasn't suicide.

He turned a grave face at me. "We may have found a suspect. But the rules are clear. We must have absolute proof before we can sterilize."

The rules were clear all right. Any practitioner of magic— be it spell-turner or elf or something else— who used magic to kill another being was to be rendered sterile, that is, magic-less. My mother always told me the procedure was extremely painful so that was enough of a deterrent for most. Still, there were some who couldn't seem to stop themselves from dabbling in the black arts.

"Absolute proof," Gran repeated. "You don't have it?"

The elf sighed again. "Unfortunately, no. We've been unsuccessful in our attempts to retrieve a power focus," he said with a frown.

"What's a power focus?" I found myself asking. I felt distinctly left out of a conversation I was very much a part of, and my frustration meter was rising.

"You don't know?" He seemed surprised. "You're weeks away from coming into your powers and you don't know what a power focus is? Alberta, how can this be?"

Gran frowned, wrapping her cardigan around herself. "She refuses to learn the old ways." She flicked flecks off her sleeves, refusing to meet the elf's gaze.

"You're not taking magic lessons?" he asked.

It sounded like an accusation. I couldn't believe it. "I'm taking magic lessons. They're not taking to me."

The elf studied me for a moment, probably trying to decide what to make of the bitterness in my voice and if I was telling the truth. The sight of his pointed ears was making me uncomfortable. I adjusted my position on the couch, wiping my palms across the soft cotton.

He sucked in a breath that was nearly a sigh. "I see. Higher level spells require an object to channel the energy, center it, focus it to where the practitioner wants it to go," he explained, settling back into the rocking chair by the window.

"Like a funnel."

"Exactly," he nodded and smiled. "Each focus is unique to the practitioner. It might be traditional like a wand or more appropriate to the task, like the wooden spoon your Gran uses. When we have the focus, we will be able to read a log of the spells that passed through it. It will also tell us who used it. It will be enough to get the sterilization."

"So why don't you go get it?" I asked. It seemed pretty simple to me.

"We've tried."

"Try harder." I found myself getting angry at him for giving up so easily.

He closed his eyes and appeared to be struggling with his words. "It's not that simple."

"You're the Council. This is your job."

"We know the location of the focus, but it's contained behind walls encrypted with the highest level of black magic we've ever seen." He grimaced. "Filthy stuff," he said to Gran with a shudder.

Gran shook her head and shifted on the chesterfield to hide her own shudder.

Black magic was rightfully shunned by the magic community, and yet there were still practitioners drawn to its powers. Black magic was the only magic acquired by choice. It required the practitioner to turn away from the magic of birth, in order to study the ways of the dark path, to use death as fuel for the spell.

There was always a choice, my mother had told me. Always.

"So sneak in," I suggested.

"That, my dear Melantha," the elf said with a smile, "is what we were hoping you would help us with."

CHAPTER THREE

"NO!" GRAN SAID immediately. "Absolutely not! I won't allow it!"

He tilted his head to the side. "Certainly it is your right to protest, but the proposition comes from the Council."

"No," I said swiftly, though not as firmly as Gran. I took a seat next to her on the chesterfield. It might have been the first time we'd agreed on anything, even if it was for very different reasons. Gran didn't want me do it because she didn't think it would be safe. I didn't want to do it because it would mean I was doing the work the lazy Council didn't feel like doing.

A look was exchanged between Gran and the elf, about what I couldn't say exactly. They had a conversation with their eyes. Gran appeared to regret having to stand up to him, but she didn't change her position. Ethelwulf's gaze shifted to his feet, seemingly also sorry about something. There was more here than the news he delivered. There was history as well. A history I knew nothing of.

"I see," Ethelwulf said resignedly. "Might I trouble you for a cup of tea? I have travelled quite a long way."

"No trouble at all," Gran said, rising. "Though you exaggerate the length of your journey. Council members are permitted to use the portals."

His eyes twinkled. "You are, of course, correct, Alberta. Still, I am such a long way from home."

"All the way from Montreal," Gran chuckled. "By alacroport."

Alacroport was the spell used to access the portals. Travelling by such method had been shut down for last several decades so the Council could confine spell-turners to using traditional human methods of travel lest we give ourselves away to humans.

See, I have been paying attention to my spell lessons.

The elf sat there smiling at me while Gran worked in the kitchen. He asked me about school and then he asked me about my friends.

"I'm not allowed to have friends," I replied, watching his reaction. Was it normal for almost-turners to go without friendship? Or was this my own private hell?

He seemed surprised to hear it at first, but then his expression changed like he remembered something. "Yes, yes," he said, nodding. "I'm not sure your mother was right about that, but she kept you alive this long." He smiled.

I was sure he meant it as a compliment to my mother's parenting, though it sounded like a criticism. Maybe he was hinting I should appreciate her strict rules. But I wasn't sure about that. It seemed he didn't exactly agree with my circumstances, whatever his reasons were.

But he did confirm one thing: my life was not normal. Other almost-turners had friends. And freedom.

"Looks like the rest will be up to you," he said as Gran came over with a tray filled with all the things for coffee and tea, and a Sara Lee cake from the freezer.

His words weren't meant for Gran. His words were fair warning of what was to come.

While I poured two cups of tea, and one coffee, Gran sliced the cake.

"You should have paid more attention to your mother's recipes, Alberta," he said with a good-natured smile, passing his fork through the store-bought cake.

"Perhaps I should have," she agreed, sitting back with her own piece. "She was a good hearth turner."

'Hearth turner' was old-fashioned, friendly slang for earth turner, so dubbed because they often spent their time gardening, cooking and baking their spells. Before there were such things as stoves and ovens, they'd spent a lot of their time at the hearth.

The two shared a smile over bleached white cake, and again I had that feeling of an unspoken history.

Once the plates were void of anything but crumbs, and the topic of the weather had been discussed at length, we sat back with our steaming cups. Apparently Ethelwulf had more to say.

"Tell me, Melantha, how well did you know your mother?"

I didn't answer. How does one answer such a question? Either I knew her well, and he would prove me wrong with his next statement, or I didn't know her at all, and he would prove me right. Wasn't that how this question goes? I tucked my feet under me, pulled the crocheted afghan over my legs, sipped my tea and waited.

Gran watched him with a wary eye over the brim of her coffee cup.

"All right," he said finally, defeated by my silence. "Did you know she was working for the Council?"

Gran studied the dark swirls in her coffee cup. Though she spoke no words, she said volumes.

I met the elf's gaze. "No," I replied, "though it seems Gran did."

"Ah, well," he said softly, as if it would take the harshness out of the news, "I didn't mean to open a family feud."

"Oh, but you did, Ethelwulf," she interjected, putting her cup on the table. "Or you wouldn't have mentioned it. As I told you before, the answer is no."

He gave her a sad smile. "And as I mentioned before, the choice is Melantha's."

Gran stood up. "That does it, Ethelwulf, I want you to leave."

He shook his head sadly. "I'm sorry, Alberta. I'm here on official Council business. You cannot ask me to leave until my business has concluded. You know that."

She flopped down to the couch, as though he'd struck her. "Don't do this. Please. I beg of you. She's all I have left."

"I'm sorry," he repeated. And it seemed to me he meant it, which worried me all the more.

"Wait," I interjected, feeling a few steps behind in this conversation, though it was about me. "Do what? What's going on?" He was upsetting Gran and I didn't like it.

Ethelwulf turned his regretful eyes on me. "I'm here to ask you to assist us."

"And I already gave you my answer. What's the problem here?"

"Your response cannot be registered until all the conditions have been met."

"Oh, I see. Elf politics."

We lived in Ottawa. I wasn't surprised to hear the old bat had an agenda. Everybody had an agenda in this city.

"Council politics," he said firmly. "I am here today to give you as much information as I am permitted. I will return at another time for your answer."

I rolled my eyes. Elf, Council, did it matter? It was all political bull crap. "And if I still say no?"

"If you can still say no after what I have told you, that will be your choice."

"Again with the choices."

"There is always a choice, my dear Melantha."

I said nothing. He sounded so much like my mother it hurt.

"Ethelwulf . . ." Gran begged.

"I am sorry, Alberta, but my hands are tied by the Council."

Gran didn't want this done, and it was sounding like a good idea to me. It seemed even the elf didn't want this done.

"So don't do it," I suggested. "Don't say another word. Just deliver my answer as no."

Gran looked at him hopefully.

"Again, I'm sorry, dear. But the rules are fixed. As your grandmother well knows."

Gran dropped her head, sagging with defeat.

"To go against Council," he continued, "would be to experience a torture that would leave one wishing one was dead."

I thought then of the invisible barrier that wouldn't let me escape to my room. Ethelwulf had said I couldn't leave until the Council's business was concluded. I had a bad feeling he wasn't the lying type.

"I've no right to ask anyone to bear that burden," Gran said. "Oh, Melantha, I am so sorry you have to go through with this."

"Enough with being sorry," I growled with frustration. "Just get this over with."

"Oh, no," she moaned.

I frowned. "As I understand, he has to tell me or else he'll be tortured. And I have to listen or else I'll be tortured." I turned to the elf. "Am I right?"

He nodded. "Exactly right."

I shrugged. "So let's just get this over with. And talk straight this time. No more of this dithering around the subject to save feelings. Truth. Now."

"Very well." He gulped down the last of his tea, and leaning on his cane, put his empty cup on the tray. He leaned back in the chair and began, "Your mother, as I said, was working for Council. We had need of a turner, someone who could get close to other turners, sorcerers, and warlocks in this area. Someone who was not identified as being on Council."

"An undercover agent?" My mother was an undercover agent? This had to be a joke. Gooseflesh broke out on my arms as if the air itself wanted to confirm what my mind refused to believe.

"Precisely. An undercover agent. Her job was to get close to black spell practitioners and bring us their focuses— er, would that be foci? Oh dear, I have such trouble keeping up with the lingo."

"Both are correct," Gran said, waving her hand. Her face held a pained expression. "Now carry on."

"Yes, well, that's the background," he said. "Last year, Lavinia was assigned to get the focus from Gerrard Lebrun. He was long suspected of using black spells, but we had yet to prove it."

"He killed her?"

"We believe so. We believe he learned her true intentions and could not risk being caught."

I'd watched enough TV to know they didn't have much by human standards: motive, suspicion. But no proof. That's why they wanted the power focus. They wanted the smoking gun.

"So what does this have to do with me? You can't be so stupid to think I would succeed up against a powerful sorcerer when my mother failed, can you?"

"Melantha!" Gran scolded, but I felt no shame. If they were asking what it sounded like they were asking, they deserved it.

The elf only smiled. "Not at all, my dear Melantha. Lebrun has a son. His name is Savion. He happens to attend your school. He happens to be in your grade."

"Yeah," I said, the image of the quiet, studious boy coming to mind. "I know who he is."

He was the kid everyone made fun of, and no one wanted to be around.

"Perfect. We want you to become friends with him. We want you to get inside his home and bring us the focus."

"Yeah, right." I snorted. "That won't be suspicious at all."

He nodded. "Indeed, this task does require subtlety, a gentle hand, for Savion is as much a sorcerer as his father."

"No way!" I choked on a laugh. I couldn't help it. The idea that wimpy kid was a sorcerer was hysterical.

The elf smiled knowingly. "He is. He will come into his powers a few months after you do."

"If his father is anything like him, then you have nothing to worry about. Even Gran could take him in a fight."

"Melantha!" Gran said, sounding shocked again.

"Oh, I assure you, he's nothing like his father," Ethelwulf said.

"Huh." It suddenly dawned on me. "Was he involved in— " I couldn't bring myself to suggest it.

I didn't need to. He knew what I meant. "Uncertain."

I nodded. There was a lot about my mother's death that was uncertain and surprising. I'd need a week just digest it all.

"So that is the task Council puts before you. You have until I return to decide."

"Can I ask a few questions?"

He gave a slight nod. "You may. I will answer to the limits I am allowed."

"Will I need to use magic?"

"Melantha!" Gran interjected. "You cannot be thinking of doing this!"

"Gran, I can't make a decision without all the facts," I said calmly, turning to the elf.

"I've heard you've all but shunned magic, despite how it upsets your grandmother. I suppose that is your choice. I'm not here to change your mind on the matter. I don't believe magic will be required to gain access to Lebrun's household."

I nodded. "What does this focus look like?"

"We are uncertain," the elf said. "Our last communication from your mother suggested she believed it was an item Lebrun kept near him. An umbrella, perhaps. But she hadn't determined that for certain."

Great. So I had to unravel a mystery not even my mother could unravel.

My next question was the important one. "How am I supposed to do this when I'm not allowed to have friends?"

He cast a gaze at Gran. "I suppose your grandmother would have no choice but to allow you to see friends for this to work. That is, if you choose to accept this quest."

"Good to know," I said, "but that's not quite what I meant. I have this sort of reputation for not having friends, for being a loner. Comes with the territory when you've been home-schooled your whole life. So how am I supposed to make friends with Savion without it seeming completely suspicious?"

I intended for the question to stump the old elf. He knew very little about kids my age and what our life was like. If anything would show him the ridiculousness of this quest, the matter or making friends would be it.

He seemed to consider my words, my situation, and then he said, "You will find that common ground will be a good place to start. Savion lost his mother a few years ago."

His words practically stunned me. First, I find out Savion was a sorcerer, and now to find out he, too, lost his mother. How could I have so much in common with this kid and not know it?

"I think that's enough for now, Ethelwulf," Gran said, standing. "You've done enough damage for one day." He opened his mouth to speak, but Gran cut him off. "Save your apologies! If she doesn't get through this, you're going to need them!"

Nodding, and using his cane for support, he got to his feet. "Thank you for the tea, Alberta. Your company has been delightful as usual," he said as he hobbled to the door. "Melantha, you have been given three days to make your decision. After that, I'll be in touch." He put his hat on, and with a final wave, the old elf left.

I needed to move, to do something. The elf's visit left me with my hands shaking, and I didn't want to stop to think about it any more. I picked up the tea tray with all the dishes, and carried it out to the kitchen. Gran followed.

"You don't have to help them," she said with venom on the last word. "They'll find another way to get the focus."

I flipped on the hot water, added the soap and began washing. "Gran, I must be their best chance or they wouldn't be asking." Not that I was saying yes.

She picked up a wet plate and wiped it with a tea towel. "There's got to be another way. There's always a choice." Her words rang with begging and pleading.

I wondered if my mother would have agreed. If there had been another way, why did she choose to risk her own life?

Was this what their big fight had been about? Gran had argued with her to stay out of Council business? Hmmm. It fit with the mysterious glances that had passed between Gran and Ethelwulf.

I spent the rest of the evening on my bed reading a novel but not seeing the words. The rocking chair creaked a steady rhythm where Gran crocheted squares for an afghan. Memories of my mother occupied both our thoughts, no doubt.

I wanted some time to mull over the Council's proposition. I'd told Ethelwulf I wasn't doing it, but the fact was, I was starting to come around on the idea. Getting rid of Gran for a while would be nice, but there was something else bothering me: Savion. I just couldn't make sense of him as a sorcerer. Kids at school picked on him terribly, and yet he rarely defended himself. How could someone like that have a black-spell sorcerer for a dad?

Unfortunately, there was no way I'd be able to make friends with Savion without raising his suspicions. It just wasn't going to happen. Plus, there was every possibility Savion's father might recognize me as my mother's daughter, and I had no plans to die anytime soon. I needed all the time I could get to think of a decent excuse to give Ethelwulf when he returned.

Of all the things the elf said today, the one that bothered me most was the suggestion that I didn't really know my mother. I'd always suspected my mother of living a secret life. She never came out and told me, but I knew it just the same. It had to do with her sending me to Gran's for four months a year. It was in her eyes before she went to work in the morning. It was in the evenings when she worked late, and in the pauses before she told me her excuses. A child knows when her mother is lying as much as a mother knows when her child is hiding the truth.

The elf knew my mother worked for Council. Gran knew. I'd always assumed my mother would one day tell me the truth, once I was old enough.

A parent shouldn't die until they've told all their secrets to their child. Everything. From their first date to how to rock a baby to sleep to where to hide the Christmas presents and what to wear on graduation day under that ridiculous gown.

Everything.

Anything less just wasn't fair.

CHAPTER FOUR

MY MOTHER USED to say I was attracted to the impossible. She would say that whenever I asked about where our powers came from. I knew the magic was inside us, but I wanted to know exactly how and where the power was created. This was probably about the time when I learned about the body's systems in my school lessons. Like the cardio-vascular system that pumped blood through our veins. I wanted to know where the magic system was, but answers were never given.

I preferred to think I enjoyed a challenge. For example: mornings. I used to get out of bed with plenty of time to spare in the morning. These days I liked to squeeze in as much sleep as I could before I had to leap out of bed. I had it down to twelve minutes if I showered. Five, if I didn't. It's all about the challenge.

After a night of tossing and turning, I opted for the five minute rush. Two and a half minutes to get dressed and brush my teeth. Two and a half minutes to grab breakfast and lunch.

"Bye, Gran," I called. I tossed my backpack over my shoulder and picked up my travel mug.

"Melantha, please be careful," she warned, pleading with her gray eyes.

"I'm going to school, Gran. Not war."

She started to say something, but changed her mind. "Promise me you'll stay away from that sorcerer boy."

I thought about it for a half a second. "We're in the same grade, Gran. I can't promise that."

"Melantha!"

I sighed. I so didn't have time for this. "Don't worry. We don't have any of the same friends."

I finished a muffin on the elevator ride down, and sipped hot coffee from a travel mug as I hurried along the busy sidewalk in the crisp morning air.

Through the night, I'd come to decide Lebrun wasn't worth risking my life for, and I was absolutely certain my mother wouldn't want me in danger. She spent her life— gave her life— keeping me safe. No way would she want me sneaking into Lebrun's house, not even to catch her killer. No matter what else had happened between us, I owed her at least that much, right?

Then there was the consideration of Savion's involvement. If he did play a part in my mother's death, how I was I ever to be friends with him? And if he didn't, if he knew nothing of his father's activities, how could I be friends with someone so obtuse? He had to know of the black magic. He just chose to do nothing about it.

I couldn't fake friendship. I'd had very few friends in my life. I'd have to either be a real friend to him or not be a friend at all.

Sir John Sparrow David Thompson Secondary School was an ancient piece of pseudo-Gothic architecture. Made of gray stone, it had a dark, ominous presence with a lot of pointy features. When I was small, I thought it was a castle, and even today, though the building was not so big anymore, part of me still wished I was attending school in a castle. The school was really pretty in the fall when the old maple trees turned bright red and orange, but now, blanketed in snow against an overcast sky, it was just cold and foreboding on this the first day of the winter semester.

"You made it."

I pulled my head out of my locker to find Rory standing beside me.

"Nice shirt," I said.

His electric bass guitar was zipped inside a soft case and strapped to his back. He wore faded jeans and a threadbare Rolling Stones t-shirt.

"I'm sorry I missed your gig last night," I said.

Rory shrugged. "You didn't miss anything. We played a bunch of old songs for a bunch of old guys."

Rory played bass in a band that specialized in classic rock. And if Rory's playing was anything to go by, then I knew they were good, too, but it would have been nice to hear them for myself.

"Aw, man. I'm really sorry," I said again.

He smiled. "Shut up already. If your Gran is anything like my Aunt, then there's one thing I totally understand."

"What's that?" I tossed my backpack over my shoulder and started in the direction of my first class.

"You can't always get what you want," he sang.

I laughed. That was Rory. He always knew the right thing to say. Which was part of why I liked hanging out with him.

"But if you try sometimes," he sang as we parted ways at the end of the hallway, "you just might find you get what you need."

It was hard to get the song lyrics out of my head, but harder to stop hearing his voice when I should have been listening to my teachers.

I didn't see Rory again until lunch time. He waited for me at our usual table in the cafeteria. As long as the weather was good, we had plenty of space because most kids walked down the road for pizza and burgers.

While he filled me in on his morning classes, I checked my lunch bag. Gran sent me with a green apple, yogurt, shredded chicken on rye bread, and oatmeal chocolate chip cookies. I started with the cookies.

"What do you know about Savion Lebrun?" I asked. I brushed a lock of hair off my forehead.

Rory smiled. "Why? You interested?"

I snorted. "Hardly."

Rory and I were just friends. For now. But I wished we could be something more. And sometimes I thought maybe he did too, but I was still waiting for some sign that he was interested.

"I heard his mother died a few years ago," I said softly. Rory glanced at me and all joking was put aside. Our own losses were still too raw.

I didn't expect him to know much more about Savion than I did since we were both new to the school, but I'd thought maybe he'd heard something. Rory didn't seem like the gossiping type, but kids will talk regardless of who might be listening.

A crash by the doors captured my attention. At the source of the crash was Savion, scrambling to pick up his books and papers.

"Speak of the devil," Rory said.

Savion was a short, scrawny kid, all skin and bones under designer-label clothing that fit too loose. His dirty blond hair needed to be cut, with the bangs falling in front of his eyes. No matter how he styled it, he couldn't disguise how sparse and thin his hair was. No matter how expensive his clothing, shoes, haircut or glasses, he seemed to have a dishevelled and awkward appearance.

The guys who had run into him stood there laughing, and as I looked around, I realized Rory and I were the only people in the entire cafeteria not snickering at Savion.

Maybe because we knew what it was like to be an outsider. Maybe because we knew what it was like to lose a mother. Either way, we watched in silence as he gathered his books and heaped them onto a nearby table.

I couldn't get over the fact that Savion was the son of a sorcerer. I so did not see that coming. I didn't know much about sorcerers. Just that they were much the same as spell-turners, but where turners were always female, sorcerers were always male, and their powers passed from father to son.

"What's his deal?" I asked, and then bit into my apple. The girls at Savion's table shook their heads as they got up and left.

Rory shrugged. "I don't know. I don't get why kids pick on him. From what I've seen he's really smart, doesn't cause trouble."

"I'm guessing he's not into sports. Does he belong to any clubs?"

"Why would I know?" Rory asked. I sensed his defences coming up.

If I took Ethelwulf's job, Savion would probably come up more in conversation, and I didn't know how I was going to hide my sudden interest in the school's outcast.

"I just feel sorry for him," I said, twisting the wrapper from my cookies into a long plastic rope.

"Whatever. I don't care about his extracurricular activities." He didn't say it, but his tone definitely conveyed his hope the conversation was over.

I shrugged again. "I was just curious." I pulled over my lunch bag. "Want my sandwich?"

"Thanks." He pulled the plastic wrap off and took a bite.

Befriending Savion was going to be even harder than I thought. If I took the job from Ethelwulf, I would have to make friends with Savion in secret. I didn't want Rory to be hurt.

Of course, I didn't have to take the job at all. Saying no would make Gran happy and get her off my back for a while.

I watched in silence as a group of seniors laughed and shoved each other— all to distract from the one kid who knocked Savion's stack of books to the floor again.

There was something odd about Savion. He just sat there eating his lunch as if nothing had happened. No matter how often kids picked on him, he always remained so calm.

"How can he just sit there like that?" I wondered out loud.

"Martial arts," Rory said, biting into the second half of the sandwich.

I smiled. "What? Is that a new way to say 'this sandwich is good'?"

He gave me a wry smile. "I heard Savion's into martial arts."

"Oh." I raised my eyebrows. I guess that might explain his calmness.

"Big into it. He made the competitive team, has medals and trophies and stuff."

"Oh." Interesting. "But if he's that good. . ."

"Why isn't he kicking everyone's ass when they knock him down?"

"Yeah." There was something curious about this boy.

***

Turns out, Savion was in my history class. So was Rory. And thanks to Mr Davis's seating plan, Rory sat on the other side of the room, while Savion sat across the aisle from me.

This was going to be a cheery semester.

Rory and I parted ways at our lockers. He had to hurry to catch a bus to get home. I had to hurry so Gran didn't have panic attacks because I was ten seconds late.

I was about to push open the front doors of the school, when through the window I saw Savion standing on the front steps. I paused with my hand on the door. Normally, I would have ducked my head and walked right past him without giving him a second thought. But now. . . I watched as he slowly descended the stairs. A group of senior boys came up behind me. I moved over. They pushed the doors open. As they went down the stairs, one of them tripped Savion and sent him sprawling to the snow-covered sidewalk. They laughed and kept on walking.

The next thing I knew, I was down the stairs and picking up the backpack that belonged to the son of the sorcerer who killed my mother.

Savion appeared to be okay. He'd rolled over and pushed himself back to his feet. Without a word he took the backpack out of my hands.

"Why do you let them do that?" I asked. "Why don't you run?"

He brushed snow off his jacket. "Why does the tiger chase the gazelle?"

Because it runs. Yeah, everyone knew that. Just as everyone knew if Savion ran the bullies would chase him. But that wasn't what I was asking.

"I mean, why do you let them do that when you have the power to stop them?" My tongue tripped over the word 'power'. I felt my cheeks flush. I didn't want him to know I knew he was an almost-sorcerer. "You know martial arts, right?"

He looked me in the eye, then. "Is that what you think power is? Beating people up?" he asked. He sounded offended. Or disappointed.

Or like he was better than me.

I didn't think power was about beating people up. Well, maybe I did. A little. Those bullies needed to be stopped. If it took someone bigger and badder to stop them, then so be it.

He suddenly straightened his shoulders and peered at me with interest. "You—"

"What?" I expected to hear about how I was stupid for my theories on power, etc., but he didn't say anything more.

"Nothing," Savion said, but I didn't believe him.

"What?" I asked again, but he didn't stick around to elaborate. Savion brushed snow off his legs and left me standing in the sidewalk watching after him, wondering what he'd been about to say.

There was something very curious about that sorcerer boy.

CHAPTER FIVE

THEY SAY HOME is where the heart is. I thought I knew my home pretty well, having lived in the same apartment in Ottawa since my father died. I figured I knew it well enough to know my heart wasn't in it.

There is a house not far from the apartment building, a two-story brick house with a red maple in the front yard, and a tree fort in the back. I skinned my knees on the street, Willow Lane, learning to ride a bike. The green grass was cut every Thursday night when my father got home because weekends were for drinking lemonade on the back patio, not listening to lawnmowers. The leaves of that red maple weren't as pretty as the bright sugar maple, but they were still great for raking up and jumping in. After the first wet snow fall, my father and I would roll up a snowman to stand under the leafless branches of the maple tree, while my mother made us hot chocolate and cookies.

The elevator doors dinged, and I stepped into our hallway. Gran was right. This was my mother's place.

My heart was buried under that red maple tree.

Gran was on the chesterfield with the TV remote in one hand and the phone in the other, engrossed in what she was watching. The news channel blared a live report of the investigation into missing politicians and the impact this would have on the upcoming election. The investigation had been going on for the better part of a year now. The story was still top news in one way or another. This city was all politics all the time.

Gran heard the door close and in the blink of an eye, her expression changed from startled to relieved to puzzled to angry.

I closed the door, dropped my backpack on the floor and proceeded with kicking off my boots, shaking off snow and hanging my coat. Bypassing my cold supper on the table, I went to the fridge. Because the province brought in time-of-use pricing for electricity, Gran always made dinner before peak time, so when I got home, it was always cold.

"What are you doing?" Gran asked. She got up and followed me, hovering near the kitchen. She still had the phone and remote in her hands. Behind her, the TV continued its evening broadcast of doom and gloom.

"Looking for something," I replied, closing the fridge and opening the freezer. It was one of those harvest gold fridges, ancient. It came with the apartment.

"What are you looking for?" Gran asked, sounding frustrated. She wasn't the only one feeling that way.

"I don't know," I said with a sigh. I shut the freezer and started opening cupboards. Nerves, frustration, and a bunch of emotions fluttered under my skin.

"What do you mean you don't know?"

"I mean, I – don't – know." Honestly, I wanted something. I just wouldn't know what it was until I saw it.

"But you're rifling through everything. You must have some idea of what you're looking for."

I shrugged, wondering if I should pull over a chair so I could see what was stored at the back of the top shelves.

I'd glanced into every cupboard and formulated a vague notion of what I wanted. Now where had I seen it?

"If you tell me," Gran continued, sounding half mad, half worried, "I can help you find it."

"I could find it myself if you hadn't changed everything," I snapped.

"You don't even know what you're looking for!" she shouted, throwing her arms up.

Frustrated, defeated, I flopped onto a chair, leaving the cupboard doors in various states of openness. I picked up my fork and stabbed at a cube of boiled potato. I was so sick of boiled potatoes. My mother always refused to boil potatoes. She'd mash them, bake them, fry them. Anything but boil them. She always said it was because she'd had them boiled too often when she was growing up. Though I'd occasionally wanted to have boiled potatoes over the years, I was kind of getting her point now.

"I hate boiled potatoes," I said with a groan.

"Melantha . . . " she started, but I cut her off.

"Don't call me that. I hate it. It's Mel." I got up and went to the fridge for the ketchup.

She huffed, clucked her tongue, and headed back to the chesterfield. "I don't know who you are anymore."

I rolled my eyes and doused my cold potatoes and meatloaf with ketchup. I could have warmed my dinner in the microwave, but I didn't feel like it.

As I mashed canned peas with my fork, I heard Gran on the phone.

"Constable Wakefield, please." There was a pause. "Yes, this is Alberta Caldwell calling back. My granddaughter has returned home. Yes, thank you. Have a good night."

I threw down my fork. "Was that the police? Did you call the cops on me?"

Gran turned her nose up. "Well, I didn't know where you were."

"I'm fifteen minutes late! It's snowing outside! You shouldn't have called the cops!"

"You should have called." She switched off the TV and put the phone on the table.

"What for?"

"To tell me you were going to be late, of course." Gran came back into the kitchen where she picked up her untouched dinner and put it in the microwave.

My eyes bulged. I could not believe it. I stared at the food on my plate until the colours blurred into a dirty Christmas patchwork. If I'd stopped to call, I would have been in trouble for wasting time for stopping. Where exactly did she expect me to call from? I didn't have a cell phone.

"Maybe you should slap a remote tracking device on me," I announced glumly.

The microwave beeped, and she sat down with steam rising off her plate.

"Don't tempt me," she said. "You should have called."

I shoved back my chair and jumped to my feet. "What difference would it make? You won't let me go out with my friends! The only places I can go without you are school and the bathroom!" I stomped over to the chesterfield, snatched up the remote. I flopped down and flipped through the channels. In the kitchen, Gran ran water to wash dishes.

After a while she came over to the living room wiping her hands on a tea towel.

"Melan—Mel," she corrected, catching herself. The shorten version of my name just sounded wrong, but I wasn't about to ask her to go back to saying my whole name again. "Did something happen today?"

"Hell, no. Everyone calls the cops when someone is fifteen minutes late," I mumbled, rolling my eyes.

She clucked her tongue, but didn't say anything about my language. "You've not been yourself since Ethelwulf was here. Did something happen with that sorcerer boy today?"

I probably should have said something like, "Gran! We go to the same school. Stop making a big deal." Instead, I muttered under my breath, "Dammit. I should have known that's what this was about."

Wouldn't you know she heard me?

"I've had quite enough," Gran said. "You're going to summon Ethelwulf, and we will settle this right this minute!"

I stared in horror as she stormed to the kitchen, opened the fridge and pulled out my unfinished spell.

"Come here and finish turning this spell," she demanded.

I'd been dreading this moment. I clamped my mouth shut and turned my attention to the TV, though I wasn't really watching it. I had to think of a way to avoid this. I wasn't ready to give my answer to Ethelwulf. And there was no way I was ready to turn a spell.

"Melantha Caldwell. I am speaking to you. You will come over here, and finish this spell."

"Gran, Ethelwulf said I could have some time to think," I said, feeling a rise of panic. I wasn't ready to deal with this. Not now.

But as much as I didn't want to turn that spell or any spell, I could feel the call of magic under my skin. It wanted to move. It wanted to turn.

I clenched my jaw and pushed the magic back down, even as I did I knew I would have to answer the call eventually. But not now. I wasn't ready.

"Melantha, finish the spell."

I switched off the TV and went to the kitchen, telling myself I wasn't being called by the magic. "Gran, he said I could have time to think about it," I repeated when she ignored me.

"Why won't you turn the spell, Melantha?"

"I'm not ready. I need more time."

"You've had long enough. And I don't see why we need to delay informing him of your decision." She went to the cupboard and pulled out the jar of forget-me-knot. "If you won't summon that old elf, then I will."

"Gran!"

She tossed a handful of dried forget-me-not into the pot, and then turned to me with a very pointed stare. "You're not actually going through with it, are you? You against a black-spell sorcerer?"

I frowned. She'd changed her argument. I didn't like the sound of it. "Why would I do that?"

"I haven't a clue," she muttered. It sounded like she knew I'd been considering taking the assignment.

She plunged a wooden spoon into the pot and began turning the spell. The liquid below the surface started to bubble, and as each bubble popped through the surface it released some of the various scents from the mixture, and it released a bit of magic, taking on a purple and green shimmer. The air over the kitchen table became charged with static electricity, and then at last, a fine mist rose, shimmering in a cloud above the pot. Gran spoke to the pot.

"Ethelwulf? Ethelwulf Tumblevater, show yourself and speak to me!"

The mist and shadows rearranged themselves to curiously form the shape of the elf's head.

"I'm not available for a summoning at the moment," Ethelwulf's voice spoke from the talking mist. "Please leave a message, and I will –"

"Ethelwulf!" Gran scolded! "I can see you cowering behind your wardrobe! You'll not fool me!"

I leaned forward and peered over the edge of the pot. There, reflected in the water, was a room viewed from the ceiling. It was a dark room lit by a single candle and fireplace, and there, hidden between the shadows and dark walnut furniture, was the elf. He seemed to know enough to avoid the wrath of Gran, even if he couldn't hide from her.

"Come out, you coward! We want to speak to you!"

The puff of mist evaporated, and at the same time, in the image in the water, the elf stepped out of his hiding place between a tall wardrobe and a sideboard loaded with curiosities that included a shiny human skull and a stuffed pheasant. His head became enlarged and his body tiny as he peered up at us. His gaze shifted from Gran to me and back again.

Ethelwulf wore navy blue plaid flannel pajamas. I was glad Gran hadn't summoned him while he was in the shower.

"I'm actually on my way out, at the moment," he said.

"In pajamas?" Gran challenged.

"You're not the only one to summon me tonight, Alberta," he replied. His scolding tone made Gran adjust her head and shoulders slightly. I could tell she didn't want an argument with Ethelwulf. At least not one she couldn't win.

"Melantha has made her decision," Gran said.

"Is that so?" he asked, considering. "I'll be there in ten minutes."

"You have five!" Gran snapped. "If you're not here in five minutes, I'll come find you!"

He nodded and the picture in the water winked out, but not before I saw him grimace. Clearly their history indicated he'd suffered Gran's anger before, and yet, he'd come here to ask me something, knowing full well it would make Gran angry. Curious.

There was a knock at the door not two minutes after the summoning ended. Gran smiled triumphantly as she adjusted her cardigan on her way to the door.

"That was quick," she said, opening the door. "Oh."

Rory stood there, bundled in his parka. "Um, hi. Is Mel home?"

"Yes," I said at the same time Gran said, "No."

"Gran!"

"I'm sorry," Gran said to my bewildered friend. "We're expecting a guest from out of town. Melantha is grounded. She will let you know at s c h o o l   w h e n   s h e   c a n   s e e   h e r   f r i e n d s   a g a i n ."

Gran didn't add "if ever", but it was there in her tone.

I launched myself at the door. "Gran! Just let me talk to him. Five minutes."

Gran pushed the door shut and blocked it with her body. "Melantha, we're expecting a guest!"

There was a sharp rap on the door, the kind of tap that could only have been made by a cane.

"Dammit, Gran," I muttered through clenched teeth, surrendering my hold on the door knob.

"Watch your language," she scolded. "Ethelwulf," she greeted, as she opened the door again. "You are late. Come in. We have business to settle."

CHAPTER SIX

"THERE'S NOTHING TO settle," I countered. Maybe it was time Gran had a taste of my anger. I shifted my stance, just itching to get my hands on the door so I could go after Rory. If the elevator hadn't carried him away already.

"I hope I haven't travelled all this way for nothing, Alberta," the elf said, panting for breath. The cane tapped on the floor as he leaned heavily on it and made his way inside the apartment.

"You haven't," Gran said and glared at me.

As soon as Gran headed for the kitchen, I pounced on the door, and dashed outside, but only found an empty hallway. What would compel Rory to come all the way over here? He knew what my Gran was like. Hmmm. I hoped everything was okay.

"Are you going to tell me what this is about? Or leave me to guess?" The elf seemed to have regained his confidence enough to spar with Gran. Not so worried about making her angry now.

Gran moved the hand-stitched pillows aside and patted the chesterfield beside her. "Melantha, come and tell Ethelwulf your answer."

"I agreed to give Melantha time to consider her options," the elf interjected.

"She doesn't need any more time," Gran responded curtly. "She's ready to give you her answer now."

Ethelwulf sputtered. "But she has to have time to weigh her options!"

"Which she's already done!"

It seemed to me the elf believed I was siding with Gran on this matter, and he didn't seem pleased about it. Perhaps there was a reason he wanted me to take my time. Just as there was a reason Gran wasn't willing to give me any time.

"I'm sorry, Alberta, but the waiting period is required. The agreement is binding. You cannot rush this."

Gran pursed her lips, her mood spiralling down a black hole. "Well, there's no point in asking her again in several days or thirty days, Ethelwulf. Melantha will not be able to get inside that sorcerer's house as she is not going anywhere for a while. She's grounded for a month! And she will be home-schooled!"

"What!" I cried.

"Now, Alberta—" the elf started.

"I knew that school was no good," she said evenly. "You should have told me you were going to be late." She occupied herself with sweeping non-existent crumbs off the chesterfield.

"Gran!"

"I'm sorry, Melantha, but this is for your own good." She would not meet my eyes.

"No, it isn't! This is all about what you want! You don't care about what I want at all!"

"I know quite well what's been asked of you and I daresay I am shocked beyond reason Ethelwulf has the gall to ask it in the first place!"

"Now, Alberta," Ethelwulf said gently, while Gran and I stared at each other, me with tears in my eyes, her with angry fire. "I think we all need to take a moment and breathe deeply—"

"Oh, shut up, you old fool," Gran snapped. "Can't you see what you've done to us?"

The old elf's expression softened. He sighed and pushed off the chair, leaning on the cane. He muttered under his breath all the way to the kitchen, where he put on the kettle and set about going through the cupboards. From my position by the window, I could hear him complain about spell-turners and the way they organized their cupboards. I knew what he meant. I could never find anything in Gran's kitchen.

Gran got up and scolded him, telling him he ought to know better than to help himself in a white turner's kitchen. She chased him out and prepared the tea and coffee. Ethelwulf shuffled back to the rocking chair.

"This will calm her down," he said, settling his old bones into the chair. He gave me a wink.

I quirked an eyebrow. "It will?"

"Oh, yes. I am told spell-turning is relaxing for turners."

"But she's not turning spells, she's making tea," I pointed out.

"Look again. Is what she's doing now any different than when she turns a spell?"

I looked again and saw Gran drop a tea bag into a mug of hot water. She stirred it three times clockwise, then three times counter-clockwise, and then removed the bag. She took a spoonful of instant coffee and dropped it into another mug, which she turned three times clockwise and three times counter-clockwise. Her movements from cupboard to table were no different from when she summoned Ethelwulf.

He was right. The end results were different, but the process she used was the same. He was even right about her mood. I could hear her softly humming while she worked.

He smiled at me and winked again. "We will let her have her say, while we enjoy a nice cup of tea, won't we?"

Seemed an odd thing to say. I thought it obvious Gran would have her say. She always did.

As for the tea, Gran was already coming our way with the cups and a plate of cookies.

I could have gone to my room and let the adults settle this, but as long as they were going to squabble about my immediate fate, I was staying to hear about it.

The elf snickered good-naturedly about coffee lovers being unable to make a decent cup of tea. "Now, Alberta, why don't you tell me what this all about." He leaned back in the rocker and sipped the steaming cup.

"I've told you, Ethelwulf. Melantha's answer is no. Don't tell me you stayed for the tea and cookies!"

He reached forward, put down his cup and saucer, and picked up a cookie. "Wouldn't dream of it, Alberta," he said. "Let's back up a bit. Why don't you tell me what happened today?"

Gran stared at me. "Melantha," she prompted.

Oh, nice. She wanted me to get myself into trouble with the elf. Not cool. She called him here. Why did I have to explain?

I had to proceed carefully. I didn't want Gran to find out the reason I was late, even though I knew Ethelwulf would be happy I stopped to talk to Savion.

"I was later than usual," I said with a sigh.

"I see," the elf said.

"And Gran called the cops on me," I continued, being just as pointed as she was with me.

"Melantha!"

She sounded shocked. I don't know why. It wasn't like somebody else called the cops on me. Did she expect me to lie to the elf to make her look good?

"You did!" I turned back to Ethelwulf and continued, "And she sent my friend away! And she grounded me for a month!"

The elf nodded. "Yes, I was here for that last part."

Gran was ready to burst. "She is too young, Ethelwulf. Far too young for what you ask of her."

The elf remained calm, his voice remained soft, though his expression grew heavy. "Age is not a concern shared by the Council."

Gran flapped. "She cannot handle such a responsibility. She can't even call home when she's going to be late!"

"Gran!" Honestly! She really truly wanted me to wear a GPS locator so she could track my every move!

"You should have called!" Gran scolded. Again.

I couldn't help it. I couldn't hold it back any longer. My mother would never have worried like this if I was late. I burst into tears. She was going to punish me for this for the rest of my life.

"Now, Alberta," the elf interjected. "I don't suppose you've considered you may be overreacting just a bit?"

"I don't suppose I have," she retorted. "Have you ever had to wonder where a beloved child is, Ethelwulf?"

"Well—"

"Have you known the horror of losing a child?"

He seemed defeated. "I don't suppose I have, Alberta," he said softly.

Gran won that round. And she knew it.

"I wasn't asking you to change your feelings, Alberta, I merely wanted you to consider Melantha's point of view. Have you?"

She fidgeted.

"Have you considered what it is like to be chained to your home? To be without friends? As I recall you had a fair number of friends and quite a bit of freedom when you were growing up."

"That's precisely my point," Gran said. "I know exactly what trouble teenagers can get into—"

"Used to," Ethelwulf corrected. "Used to get into. Look around, Alberta. It's a new world. And Melantha is not you."

She didn't look around. She looked directly into the elf's eyes, with a pained expression on her face.

"Don't do this to her, Ethelwulf. Please. She's all I have left."

He seemed just as pained. "You are asking me to draw a curtain around the sun, my dear. The Council has chosen."

What? What did that mean? What had they chosen?

Tears fell silently down Gran's face. Her shoulders shook.

Ethelwulf picked up his cane and put his top hat on. "I'm truly sorry, Alberta."

I thought he was leaving, but he waved his cane in a wide circle that encompassed us both— me and him. There was a sharp crack, like a firecracker, and the next thing I knew, we were gone.

CHAPTER SEVEN

WE WERE SITTING at a small round table that was covered in a flower-print cloth. A vase with plastic roses sat between us, and frilly, flower-print curtains hung beside us. It was warm here, despite a cold draft lingering behind the curtains.

"Where are we?" I asked. Voices murmured all around from people seated at tables like ours, though no one seemed to have noticed we just appeared out of thin air. I smelled tea and pastries and chocolate.

"Aunt Elizabeth's Tea Room," Ethelwulf answered. "I need a decent cup of tea. Don't tell your Gran, but her tea is like dishwater."

I knew the place, it was just down the street from our apartment building, though I'd never set a foot inside.

"But, Gran—" She was going to kill me for disappearing.

"I've left her frozen in a moment of time. She doesn't even know we left."

I eyed him. "Really?"

"Really."

"So I'm not going to get in trouble when I get home?"

"Would I do that?" he answered with a devilish twinkle in his eyes and a smile on his face.

"We came here by alacroport. I thought that wasn't allowed," I pointed out.

Ethelwulf waved a hand. "Exception for Council members. We'd never get anything done, otherwise."

A waitress came over. "Welcome to the Tea Room. What can I get for you?"

"Earl Grey with lemon for me," the elf said. "And whatever the young lady would like."

I was confused. I leaned closer to the elf so he could hear me. "We just had tea at home."

He considered. "That was for Alberta's benefit. This is for ours," he said. "Order what you'd like."

I glanced up at the waitress. "I don't suppose you have hot chocolate in a place like this?" I asked.

She smiled. "I believe we do. Is that everything?"

Ethelwulf nodded, and she promised to be right back with our order.

"So my dear, you've had quite a day," he said to me.

I shrugged. He didn't say anything until after the waitress returned with our beverages.

He stirred a wedge of lemon into his tea. "I lied to your Gran, you know," he said. That caught my interest. He didn't seem like the type to lie to anyone, but especially not to Gran.

"I can take your answer whenever you are ready to give it," he explained. A cloud of expectation hung over the air we breathed.

I swallowed. No pressure or anything.

"Tell me about my mother," I said. I scooped a fluff of whipped cream off my mug of hot chocolate. This hot chocolate was so fancy it came with chocolate curls on top. I was in heaven. "Why was she working for you?"

He brought the teacup to his mouth. "I suppose her reasons were her own," he muttered quickly before sipping. "You aren't asking me to conjecture, are you?"

"Since she's not around to answer for herself, yes, I want you to conjecture," I said icily. Why else would I ask?

I expected him to get mad about my attitude. Instead, he chuckled.

"Is my dead mother funny to you?" I asked, narrowing my eyes at him. I couldn't figure this guy out. He wanted something from me, but he was laughing at me.

He sobered. "No, no. Certainly not. Your mother was a good woman. A powerful spell-turner."

"Then what's so funny?" I dared to ask, though I probably should have known better.

He sobered, and hid his smile behind the porcelain cup. "You remind me of someone."

"Who?" I asked suspiciously.

He dipped his eyebrows. "Your grandmother."

I almost choked. "Gran? Me? Are you crazy?"

"More and more every day," he replied. Though I wasn't sure if he meant he was crazy or if he was saying I was becoming more like her.

"Ugh," I grunted with frustration. "Could you just tell me about my mother, please?"

"I can't."

"Yes, you can."

"I do apologize, but I cannot tell you about her work for us, and outside of that, I'm afraid I didn't know her very well," he said, his voice heavy. "A circumstance I do regret."

"Why can't you tell me about her work? I went without a mother four months of the year— every year— because of her work for you people. You owe it to me to tell me what was so important!"

"I'm afraid her work was classified U.S. You have not been cleared by security for briefing."

"What's U.S.? American?"

"No, no. Utmost Secret. Only members of Council are read into U.S. classified files."

"I don't believe this," I muttered.

"I am sorry."

How did my mother get herself involved in secret projects? My mother who liked to put on the music of her youth and dance in the kitchen? My mother who baked birthday cakes decorated like sunflowers? My mother who made the best spaghetti sauce in the whole world?

"But Gran knows," I pointed out. "That's why she's being such a bear, isn't it? She knows what my mother was doing."

"She was cleared by security and read in when we opened the investigation into your mother's death."

"Murder," I corrected.

"Alleged," he said with an expression that reminded me they still wanted 'absolute proof'.

"So read me in," I said. I stirred my hot chocolate with the spoon, making swirls of cream on top. If I was a white turner, like Gran, I would feel a connection forming between me and the liquid. But I felt nothing.

"Are you saying you'll work for us?" he asked.

I studied his expression. The brim of his hat had left a red line across his forehead. I wished I could flip his head open and extract what I wanted to know. "Is that what it will take to find out what my mother was doing?" I asked.

We were locked in a staring contest.

"I can think of a few easier ways," he said. "You could, for example, talk to your Gran."

I sighed. "I've tried. She won't tell me anything."

He nodded. "She was sworn to secrecy. Still, she knew your mother better than anyone."

"Are you sworn to secrecy, too?"

He lifted an eyebrow. "Quite."

I stirred the hot chocolate some more, thinking. "So, if I agree to work for you, you'll tell me about my mother's work?"

"As much as I am permitted."

I was tired of playing games. "That's not what you implied before."

I waited while he put together the next excuse. Taking the job meant finding out what my mother had been doing all those years when I wasn't with her. It meant friending Savion and finding out if he was involved in my mother's death.

And it meant alienating Rory. I didn't want to upset him, so if I took the job, I had to make sure it didn't interfere with our friendship.

"I will do my best, Melantha, to give you the answers you seek," he said finally. "But you must understand, I do not control the Council."

"What do you mean? Who controls the Council?" I thought Ethelwulf was the leader of the Magic Council.

"The Elders make all the decisions for the Council. And their decisions are final."

"Who are the Elders?" Sometimes I really hated that I was so sheltered from other turners.

He sipped his tea while he chose his words. "If the Council is the magic community's police, then the Elders are the government."

So if I took the job, I might not even be paid. But something about the elf told me he was good for his word. Maybe the Elders would oppose him telling me some things, but I had a good bet Ethelwulf would tell me as much as he could.

"What about Gran?" I asked. "If I take the job, she's going to freak."

He tapped a finger on the table, thoughtful.

"Finish your drink," he said, then swallowed down the last of his tea. He stood up and pulled a gold coin out of his pocket and placed it on the table.

"You can't pay with that."

"Oh," he said, surprised. "I forgot."

He tapped the coin with the handle of his cane and the piece of gold unfolded itself into a crisp ten-dollar bill.

Neat trick. I had to get me some money like that.

I gulped down my hot chocolate that was still too hot to drink. It burned as it slid down, but I wasn't passing it up for anything.

"Are you ready?" he asked, holding out his elbow to me.

"I hope so," I said, wrapping my fingers around his arm. "Incidentally, where are we going?" I asked. There was no fancy crack and appearance somewhere else; we walked out of the tearoom.

"We're going to deal with Alberta," he said with a wink.

CHAPTER EIGHT

"BUT I DON'T have a coat," I protested as a blast of cold wind and fat, wet snowflakes hit me in a full-body assault.

"Don't you?" he asked with a hint of teasing in his tone.

"No, I—" Looking down, I saw that, indeed, I did have a coat, though I wasn't wearing one moments before. "This isn't my coat."

This was a furry-trimmed, down-filled parka in rescue orange. Way better than my old worn-out jacket.

"I know," he said casually. "This is better."

This was bribery. Anybody could see that. We were heading towards my apartment.

"You're being nice to me," I pointed out. "You really want me to take this job, don't you?"

The elf stopped. "You are our last chance. We've been unable to penetrate the sorcerer's defences. Only a human or almost-turner will be able to get through. Bringing a human into this is out of the question."

That was the second most important rule about magic: don't let the humans know about it.

Speaking of humans. . .

What would Rory think if I took the job and started talking to Savion?

Which meant if I took the job, I'd have to befriend Savion in secret. Could I do it? Would he accept a secret friendship, or would he want to flaunt the first friendship in his entire life? I know I'd want to.

I wasn't sure that was a risk I wanted to take.

But my mother's killer could go free and kill again. I wasn't sure I wanted to live knowing I could have helped capture him, but chose not to because of a boy.

There had to be a middle ground.

"I'll do it," I said, and Ethelwulf grinned. "If you agree to my conditions."

I expected him to object, maybe not on the scale of Gran's objections, but still, I was prepared for an argument. Instead, he only grinned more.

"I'm looking forward to hearing your conditions, once we are inside somewhere warm, hmm?" he said with a wink, and didn't say another word for the rest of the way.

The walk home was somehow colder and seemed to take longer than it should have. I felt happier once I was out of the blowing snow and inside our nice, warm apartment.

Then I noticed Gran. She was slumped forward in a chair, snoring. So this was what the elf meant when he said she was frozen in time.

Ethelwulf came in behind me, took off his hat and sat in his usual place by the window.

I hung up my new jacket on the coat rack, and went to flop on to the chesterfield. I pulled the afghan over my legs.

"I'm willing to bring you the focus and give you access to Lebrun's home," I said. "But I will need some help."

He seemed either amused or impressed. "What did you have in mind?"

"Gran. She doesn't let me out, and won't let me have friends. She's grounded me for a month and threatened to home school me. I won't be able to complete this assignment with her holding my leash."

"I can arrange for her to take a vacation, if you'd like," he suggested.

"That would be perfect. For how long?"

"For as long as you need."

"Can you arrange for Gerrard to take one too?" I asked hopefully.

He clucked his tongue. "I can sway your Gran not because her powers are lesser than mine, but because we have a personal connection. As proof, here I am inside her home." He frowned. "Lebrun is a black magic sorcerer. Your Gran uses her power to create. Lebrun uses his to kill. That is one power I cannot overcome."

"So you're saying he's more powerful than you?"

"Not at all. Every human has the ability to murder and yet not everyone does. Do you see?"

"Not really."

"Suffice it to say that some minds can be changed, while others cannot."

"So you'll take Gran away?"

"Correct." He stood up like he was getting ready to leave.

"I have other conditions."

"Have you?"

"I'll need money. Gran controls all the money around here. I have none and a girl's got to eat."

"Anything else?"

I shook my head. That seemed to about cover it. I would have my freedom, and that meant I could also have friends.

"Then I have a few conditions of my own," the elf said.

"Such as?" I wasn't expecting this. I'd thought working for him would be enough.

"I cannot leave you alone, unprotected, so I shall leave you with a guardian— a familiar, if you will."

He reached into the pocket of his coat and pulled out a small wooden box with a mesh window on the lid. He passed it to me, and reluctantly, I peered inside.

I gasped. "But it's a grasshopper!"

"Ahem," the insect said. "I'm a cricket. And no, the name's not Jiminy. It's Paul."

"Paul?"

"That's right. And no Beatles jokes. I hate that."

Unreal. I was talking to an insect. I gaped at Ethelwulf. "You can't be serious."

"In exchange for arranging for your Gran to be away, you will carry Paul with you wherever you go," he said solemnly. He was serious.

There goes my freedom.

"No!" I said at the same time Paul said, "What?"

"Paul, I'm counting on you to look out for Melantha Caldwell, while her grandmother is away. She needs your help."

"I do not!" I protested while the insect cried, "No way!"

Ethelwulf put on his hat and leaned on his cane. He slipped a small blue marble on the table, then tapped it with his cane. The marble turned into a bundle of twenty-dollar bills.

"Yes, I believe this will do," he said. Then he took his cane and pointed it at my grandmother. One second Gran was snoring in the armchair and the next she was gone. An orb appeared in the elf's hand and grew to be palm-sized and made of clear glass. Inside was a sandy beach, a blue ocean and Gran.

"Whoa," was all I could say. "How did you do that?"

The cricket snickered. "Council powers, how else?"

"Speaking of which, Melantha, you are now a tertiary member of Council with all the rights and responsibilities that position affords."

"What does that mean?" I had a bad feeling.

"Duh, it means you have Council powers and a job to do," the cricket chimed in.

I was really beginning to hate that insect.

"Does this mean I get a cane?" I asked.

"No," Ethelwulf answered. "You must work undercover, like your mother. Do you have a piece of jewelry you can wear every day?"

"Hold on," I said. I went to my room, to my dresser and opened the top drawer. Deep down under the socks, I found what I was looking for. I pulled it out and took it to the elf.

He held the locket in his hand, examining the pictures inside of my mother on one side and my father on the other. He nodded and tapped the locket with his cane. Satisfied, he placed it around my neck.

"I have the full powers of the Council now?" I asked.

Ethelwulf chuckled. The insect snorted.

"Not exactly," the elf said. "But you have what you need."

Ethelwulf placed his hat on his head and hobbled for the door with the orb containing Gran in his hand.

"Wait," Paul yelled. "You can't leave me here with this little turner — she's not even a full turner!"

Ethelwulf was really taking Gran away. I'd really agreed to do this thing. Panic rose with in my chest. Oh my Merlin. I had to catch a sorcerer.

"How will I know I've found the focus?" I asked, as he hobbled toward the door.

"You'll know," he said, putting on his hat and opening the door.

"How will I contact you once I've found it? I can't do a white turner's summoning spell."

"Oh, that's the easy part. You're part of Council now. Say my name, and I'll come to you." He winked and with a tip of his hat, he pulled the door shut behind him.

Wait— what did he mean that was the easy part? What was the hard part?

I ran to the door, hoping to catch him before he got to the elevator, but when I stepped out to the hallway, it was empty. The elf was gone. Just like that. Gone.

"Crap," I muttered, closing the door.

"Ditto," the cricket said.

I frowned at the box on the coffee table. "What are you complaining about? I have a cricket for a familiar!"

"I have an almost-turner for a witch!"

"It's turner, you rude little invertebrate. At least I'll soon be a full turner! You'll always be a cricket!"

It harrumphed. "If you live that long," it muttered.

"You're supposed to see that I do," I pointed out, and peered more closely at the box. "Are you sulking?"

"No!" it said too quickly. "Crickets don't sulk."

"Then you're pouting."

"Am not!" he snapped.

Okay then. Whatever. I put his box down on the coffee table and walked away.

"Aren't you going to let me out?"

"You might get stepped on."

"Do you think this is my first time being a cricket?"

"Well, it's my first time having one."

I picked up my calculus textbook and went to the chesterfield to read it. At that moment, the cricket began to sing.

You'd think being a cricket he would know a thing or two about singing. But this one, not so much. It was bad enough it was off-key, but did he have to sing pop songs? And he wasn't even singing the right lyrics! He was making up words and mumbling over other parts. I tried to ignore him, thinking if he didn't have an audience he would stop. But he just kept going. After the third Britney Spears song, I just couldn't take it anymore.

"Enough!"

"I'll stop if you let me out," he said slyly.

Knowing I would regret it, I let him out of the box. Anything for a quiet life.

I sat down again and opened workbook. I didn't even get to read so much as the first question when the stupid cricket jumped up and landed on my arm.

"So whatcha reading?" he asked. "Is it any good?"

"It's none of your business." I snapped the book shut, flicked the cricket away and stomped off to the kitchen, where I sat down and tried to do my homework again.

"Are you — always — this — grouchy?" he asked as he hopped across the room and landed on the kitchen table.

"Are you always this annoying and nosey?" I shot back.

He yawned. "Only when I'm bored."

"So find something to do."

"I already have."

"Great. Go do it."

"I am. I'm getting to know you."

"So you're the type of — thing— that gets to know people by pushing their buttons?"

He nodded. "Pretty much, yeah."

"Has the fact that I could squash you under my shoe completely escaped you?"

"Nah. But you'd have to catch me first." It laughed, thoroughly enjoying his annoying little self.

"That's it." I slammed the book shut, yet again. "You're going back into your cage."

"No!" he cried as he leaped off the table. I dove, but missed, and landed with my forearms hitting the hard floor.

"Missed me! Missed me! Now you have to kiss me!" He was poised on the back of the armchair, wagging his butt at me.

"Not on your life," I muttered. I jumped up, swept my arms in a wide arc and narrowly missed as he bounded off the chair to coffee table.

"Nyah, nyah, na-nyah-nyah," he taunted, and then back-flipped through the air, landing in the space behind the TV.

"Catch me if you can," came his muffled cry, "Almost-turner!"

"Don't need to." I reached over and closed the wardrobe doors.

"Hey!" I barely heard him through all the wood. "That's not fair!"

"You shouldn't be so annoying."

"But it's dark in here!"

"You'll get used to it."

He was quiet for all of thirty minutes. I got in one solid half hour of homework, and then he said, "So I hear you don't know how to turn spells."

Great. Ethelwulf gave me a smaller, more annoying version of Gran. And I had agreed to carry it with me.

"I know how to turn spells, thank you," I said. "They just don't work for me."

"I might be able to help with that," he offered. But I saw right through his plan. He just wanted me to let him out of the cupboard.

What could a cricket familiar possibly know about turning spells anyway? According to traditional turner lore, familiars were companions. They didn't have powers. They were thought to be souls trapped in animal bodies. Put there by a magic so black, so powerful, it couldn't be performed by a single turner. It was suspected only rogue cults of turners could make familiars. But there hadn't been a rogue cult around since the early Eighties. Was that how long Paul had been trapped inside a cricket's body?

Maybe that had something to do with why he wanted out of the box and out of the cupboard. Maybe being trapped in a tiny body for so long made one a little claustrophobic. Maybe I should let him out . . .

Just then, he went back to singing. This time, show tunes.

Forget it. He could stay right where he was.

I had my freedom, but at what price?

CHAPTER NINE

I WOKE UP when my internal clock exploded and I knew I was late. I hit the floor running, quickly changing my clothes. I grabbed my backpack, some food for the day, and raced all the way to school.

Rory was waiting at our lockers.

"You made it," he said with a smile. It was his usual greeting; I was usually late.

"Yeah," I said. I turned the combination on my lock and pulled open the door.

"I'm surprised the warden let you out this morning." His tone was mainly one of concern, but I detected some annoyance lurking below.

"I'm sorry about last night," I said, pulling out the books I needed for first and second period. "My Gran gets crazy when she's expecting company."

"It's fine."

It was anything but fine. Gran had no right to turn him away like that. She should have let me talk to him.

"I would have called," Rory said, "but I didn't know your phone number."

"Oh." I opened a notebook, tore out a blank page, and scribbled our number. "It's not listed," I said as I handed it back to him.

He took the paper, folded it and tucked it into his pocket. "I wanted to tell you we got invited back."

"For another gig?"

"For a regular gig. We're officially the on-call substitute band." Rory grinned from ear to ear.

"Awesome!"

I closed my locker, and we started walking toward our first classes.

"When do you play next?" I asked. An idea was taking shape.

"Actually, we've been called back tonight. Turns out the lead singer of the regular band doesn't have food poisoning. It's the flu. He's out for the week."

"Nice! Can I come watch you play?"

"But your Gran—"

"She's away for a few days," I ad-libbed.

"Really?"

"Just for a couple of days." I tried to be reassuring. "A neighbour is keeping an eye on me." Wow, this ad-libbing wasn't hard at all.

"And you're allowed to go out while she's away?" After the way Gran shut the door in his face, I couldn't blame him for being skeptical.

I shrugged. "She didn't say I couldn't."

"Well, all right!" He gave me the address and time.

I grinned. "I'll be there."

***

Paul had been quiet all day. I should have known this was unusual for a cricket. And for Paul.

I'd toted him around in my backpack just as Ethelwulf prescribed. I'd thought Paul would have made a nuisance of himself, chirping during class time just to embarrass me, but he didn't. I'd assumed he was sleeping.

He was even quiet when I got home. Which suited me just fine. I needed to get ready to go to see Rory play. I was really looking forward to this. The elf's mission came at just the right time. Another day with Gran around, and Rory would probably have stopped speaking to me. Now I had a chance to get to know him.

I was in the bathroom applying a coat of mascara. I don't usually wear make-up. I can't be bothered to take the time for it, and I don't know how to put it on or what colours to wear, anyway. So I should have known better than to put on mascara before going to Rory's gig.

"Hey!" Paul cried as he jumped onto the bathroom counter.

My mascara wand careened off course, sliding a streak of black across my cheek.

"What the hell! I almost took my eye out!"

"What do you mean 'what the hell'? What the hell do you think you're doing, missy?"

"Well, now I'm cleaning mascara off my face," I said bitterly. I grabbed a facecloth, ran some water over it and started scrubbing.

"You're supposed to be going to Savion's house, remember? Not hanging out with some rock and roll dude."

"Rory is not a rock and roll dude."

"He's not the son of a sorcerer either."

"Exactly. He's a nice, normal human."

"Have you forgotten you have a job to do?" Paul asked. "Ethelwulf is counting on you."

So what if he was. This was my first opportunity to go out and have fun. No way was I going to waste it.

With my face cleaned and my make-up half decent, I grabbed my coat and a small purse that had belonged to my mother. I stuffed some of the money Ethelwulf left me into my pocket. Paul hopped around the apartment, following me, blasting me with more of the same guilt trip.

Before I left, I turned and stared him right in the eye. At least as much anyone could stare a cricket in the eye. "I'm going," I said. "Are you coming or not?"

I held the purse open. His antennae twitched back and forth as he weighed the decision.

"This is a bad idea," he said. He hopped into the purse.

I snapped it shut and headed out into a wintery night in Ottawa ready for some fun.

***

The Salty Pig on Somerset Street was only a fifteen-minute walk from our apartment building. I was surprised to find out the pub was inside a renovated two-and-a-half-story, redbrick, Victorian house with a peaked roof and gingerbread trim around the porch. Climbing up the steps I had the curious sensation of not arriving at a pub at all, but of approaching the door to someone's home despite what was written on the sign out front. Inside there was no sense of the former home at all. It had been completely redesigned to an open floor plan with round tables scattered about and a stage set up in the big bay window. Rory was on the stage, setting up his guitar and equipment. He saw me and came right over.

"You made it." He grinned.

"You didn't doubt it, did you?"

"Never," he said, but I thought I detected a note of uncertainty in his voice.

I was about to question his doubts, and then thought better of it. I was probably misinterpreting him. He cared that I was here; there was no reason for me to assume he thought I wouldn't show after I'd told him I would be here. It was this job— working undercover for the Council had me on edge.

Rory held his arm up, indicating an empty table near the stage.

"It's a little close to the speakers," he said apologetically, "but at least on breaks, I'll be able to talk to you."

I smiled. "I'd like that."

Especially since I don't know anyone else here.

The crowd here was a little older, mostly couples in their forties and fifties. The more time Rory could spend with me, the better.

In spite of Paul's warnings, coming to hear Rory play wasn't a bad idea at all. I had fun at The Salty Pig. The lead singer and guitarist, Jared, was the nephew of the owner of the pub. He came out and told me Jared's friends were allowed free soft drinks all night. I ordered a Pepsi and the glass never got empty.

Rory and Jared's band was good. I already knew this from having listened to Rory and Jared play together at school during lunch breaks, but hearing them play with the rest of band and with the expectation of the crowd, they were still good.

At the end of the night, I waited around while Rory put away his guitar. Jared and the other guys were placing orders for food with the waitress, and called out to Rory for his order.

Rory looked to me. "Can you stay?"

I shook my head. "I really should get back home."

I swear I heard someone in a really quiet voice mutter, "Ya think?" Paul. I gave my purse a swat.

"I'll walk you home," Rory said.

***

Despite Paul's warnings, I went back every night for the rest of the week.

Paul had been wrong. Or so I thought. Who knew Paul would turn out to be right about something?

It happened in biology class. I'd been looking forward to this lab ever since Gran signed me up for school. Dissection wasn't a lesson my mother offered as part of being home schooled and shuttled between two homes halfway across the country.

The locust lay on its side in a black rubber-lined tray, the instruments lined up neatly beside it on the shiny black counter top. Around the room, other kids were lined up along the lab station that ran around the back and sides of the room. In the centre of the room, still seated at her desk, was the girl who'd opted not to do the dissection for personal reasons. I think she was a vegetarian and animal rights activist. She had to do a twelve-page report for next Friday instead. I was glad I'd opted for the dissection. She flipped through her report and cast glances around the room. Maybe she wished she'd chosen differently. The other kids had their books open and were happily hacking away at their insects.

I had every reason to be excited by this lab, but instead I was calculating how many pages per day I'd have to write before Friday. Every time I looked at my locust, all I could think about was Paul.

Not to mention, all morning I had this sick feeling in my stomach. It had been slowly growing on me for the last couple of days. And now I wondered if I'd physically be able to get through the dissection, or if I'd end up hurling.

"Is there a problem, Melantha?" Ms Rooney asked. Her long glossy black hair was a stark contrast against the matte white lab coat.

"No. No problem." I swallowed.

"You'd best get a move on. Most students have achieved stage three now."

I nodded and picked up the scissors, my hands trembling. She moved on to check on other students. I began to cut open the abdomen of the locust, wincing with every snip. That's when Paul made an appearance.

He crawled out from under the textbook stand, shocking the hell out of me. I gasped, and several nearby kids turned and gawked, so I quickly covered with a coughing fit. Ms Rooney gave me a concerned expression, so I smiled, waved and ducked my head back down to the topic at hand.

"Keep it down, would ya?" Paul whispered, perching his front legs on the side of the tray. His antennae swiveled and twitched. "I'd hate to get caught sneaking around in here."

"What are you doing here?" I whispered, trying to follow stage two, while also trying not to appear like I was talking to myself. Thankfully I'd chosen the station that was alone in the back corner of the room.

"I was curious."

"Don't you know curiosity killed the cricket?" I waved my hand over the tray.

"Ha. Ha," he said dryly, but he craned his neck trying to examine the insect soaked in preservatives. "Do you have a way into the sorcerer's house yet?"

"Of course not," I mumbled. It was the same question he'd asked me every day for the past week.

Gagging, I removed the locust's body wall and set it aside.

"Are you nuts? You have a job to do, remember?"

"I also have a life to live," I whispered, removing the locust's guts, completing stage two. I picked up my pencil and notebook, moving on to stage three: drawing a dorsal view of the interior of the locust.

A quick glance up revealed Ms Rooney was questioning each student on the parts of the circulatory system.

"You've got to get into Savion's place and nab the focus," Paul said, climbing into the tray. He took one look at the locust and shuddered.

"Get out of there!" I waved my trembling hand over him until he jumped out and crawled back under the bookstand.

Grimacing on the inside, I smiled at the kid next to me. "Fly," I explained helpfully.

"The teacher's coming," I whispered to Paul. I'd just finished labeling my diagram when Ms Rooney arrived to quiz me. She told me I passed the quiz, but was still falling behind in the assignment. Then she moved on.

"It's started already, hasn't it?" Paul asked.

"What has?"

"The curse."

"What curse?" I cast a glance in Ms Rooney's direction.

"The Council's Curse. If you don't fulfill your contract with Council there will be consequences."

I vaguely remembered him mentioning something like that a few days ago.

"What kind of consequences?" A waft of formaldehyde hit me right in the back of my throat, activating my gag reflex.

This time I couldn't stop it. I barely got bent over in time to empty the contents of my breakfast onto the floor.

"Those kind of consequences," Paul said. He hopped down and slipped into my backpack.

"I'll see what I can do," I whispered.

Paul poked his head out of the bag and tsked. "You'd better. You don't want to find out what happens when you break a promise to a Council member."

I apologized to Ms Rooney. She was fine with it. Apparently, I wasn't the first kid to throw up in a dissection. Judging by some green expressions around the room, I was fairly certain I wouldn't be the last.

But I felt like an idiot. I wasn't sick. It wasn't the dissection or the flu. Ms Rooney wanted to send me home. I told her it was just a reaction to the smell. But when she said I could go clean up in the washroom, I scooped up my backpack and practically ran.

I checked all the stalls to make sure I was alone. I was.

"Paul!" I opened the bag. "What happens if I break my promise?"

"You don't want to know."

"Tell me."

"You won't like it."

I grit my teething, fighting a wave of nausea. "But I need to know."

"Ever had a wart?"

I relaxed. Compared to the nausea, warts were no big deal. "Yeah. Once. On the bottom of my foot."

"Ever have green warts all over your body?"

"Ew! No!"

"Yes. And that's just the start."

So much for having a social life. Green warts would kill it. Then how would I get into Savion's house?

I absently scratched the back of my hand.

"What did you just do?" Paul asked, his voice thick with suspicion.

"What? Nothing."

"That scratching. What is that?"

I held up my hand. "Oh, no."

It was small, but unmistakable. A neon green dot had formed on the back of my hand.

I pulled my sleeve down over it.

I reached to scratch the back of my neck and stopped.

If a cricket's eyes could widen, then Paul's went huge. "You'd better get that contract fulfilled. And fast."

Paul was probably right— at least, he sounded like he was talking from experience. I decided to find Savion and somehow invite myself over to his house tonight. I just had to figure out how to do it without upsetting my new boyfriend.

CHAPTER TEN

SOMEONE ONCE SAID we are all defined by our choices. I used to agree with this, back when my choices were easy.

I hoped no one ever judged me by the choices I would make before this was all over.

At lunch Rory and Jared could be found in the music room shredding on their guitars and I usually went to listen to them play. But after finding another green dot on my arm, I decided on a change of plans.

I wandered the halls in search of Savion. If I was him, I would eat my lunch in a classroom where I could hide from the idiots. But no. Instead, I found him sitting alone at a table in the middle of the busy cafeteria.

I sighed. Really? I had to do this in front of the entire cafeteria?

I wondered if I should wait until I could get him alone. Like maybe after lunch or between classes. I didn't want to do this in front of an audience. But if I waited, I might not catch him. I had to deal with this today. If I didn't— I shuddered. I didn't want to know what would happen next.

I sucked up a deep breath, sat down in the chair across from him and pulled out my lunch. I pulled the top off a cup of yogurt and dug in with my spoon.

I thought he might object to my being there, but he didn't say a thing. Not even a 'hello'. He barely acknowledged my presence with a slight tilt of one eyebrow and kept his gaze fixed to the table.

"Nice sunny day," I commented.

Savion shrugged. "Too cold."

"That's why it's so crowded in here today," I said, as though he'd dropped in the missing piece to a puzzle.

That made him give me a look that clearly said, "Well, duh."

I smiled. "I decided you're right. I don't know anything about how to handle bullies."

Savion didn't say anything.

"That's what happens when you're home schooled, I guess," I continued. "You don't learn how to deal with difficult people because there aren't any."

Still, he said nothing. But he watched me, patiently waiting for something. Maybe for me to get to my point.

"So," I said, stirring my yogurt, "I was wondering if you could teach me."

He backed his chair up and picked up his stuff.

"Wait," I said.

"I'm not going to be the butt of your jokes," he said in a scathing tone.

"I'm not joking."

Savion stared at me for the longest time. I started to wonder if I'd broken out in green dots on my face, but I felt no itchiness. At least, not on my face. I didn't want to appear nervous, so I returned his stare, resisting the urge to run my fingers over my face to check for spots. Eventually he sat back down.

"There's nothing to learn," he said, playing with the plastic from his sandwich. "You just ignore them and they move on."

"But they don't move on from you," I said.

He seemed surprised that I had noticed.

"Maybe it's because you're so small, so skinny," I said quickly. I didn't want him thinking I'd noticed because I was interested in him. Everyone noticed Savion got picked on. It's just no one ever said anything to him about it.

"Have you thought about weightlifting?" I asked. "You know, to bulk up?"

He pushed his chair back, and this time, he didn't stop when I said wait. He left me alone, and I felt more than saw the curious stares of the other kids.

This job was impossible, thanks to Savion's antisocial nature.

How in a hag's name was I going to get him to trust me enough to invite me to his house?

***

Everything got worse when I arrived at history class. But by the end of the day, I would look back at lunch and history class and know they weren't the worst part of the day. No, the worst was still to come.

Rory came into the history classroom and made straight for my desk when he saw me.

"Where were you at lunch?" he asked. His tone was light, but carried undercurrents of concern.

I shrugged, trying to keep things light. "I ate at the cafeteria today."

No point in lying. Plenty of kids saw me in the caf today. Someone would tell him so.

"Are you sick of me already?" Rory smiled, but the undertones were still there.

"Of course not," I said. "I forgot my lunch and had to buy something. And I didn't feel like walking all the way back to the music room."

I put a little tone in my voice to let him know I was annoyed with the questions. Rory got the hint.

"I just missed you, that's all," he said.

I smiled. "I'll come watch you practice tomorrow," I promised.

Little did I know then I wouldn't be able to keep that promise.

Mr Davis cleared his throat, and Rory went to his seat on the other side of the room.

I didn't like the undertones in Rory's voice. It wasn't his words I objected to, it was all the things he wasn't saying. Like he didn't trust me or something. Like there was any reason for him to be jealous of Savion.

Maybe he did miss me and I was being too harsh. I'd rather have spent the lunch hour with him. I liked hanging out with him and I wished we could spend more time together.

But I had these dang green spots to contend with. I pulled up my sleeve and examined the one on the back of my hand. The thing had nearly doubled in height and itched like mad around the edges where the colour had gone turquoise.

I had to get rid of them. But the only way I could was to fulfill my contract with the Council. And to do that, I had to get the Council into Savion's house.

I suddenly became aware of chairs sliding on the floor and bodies moving around. I'd zoned out and missed the instructions on what we were to be doing right now.

"What are we supposed to be doing?" I asked Savion.

He rolled his eyes.

Across the room Jared was occupying Rory in some conversation, while Rory stared at me like he was sorry. Kids were sliding desks together, so I couldn't even go over and ask Rory what we were supposed to be doing.

"Okay, so that's it then," Mr Davis said. "Everyone has a partner. I suggest you get started, since it's due tomorrow."

"Wait— What?" I was completely lost.

Kids chuckled.

"Pull up a chair, Ms Caldwell," Mr Davis said. He slapped a handout on Savion's desk. "Time to get started."

"Um— I'm not Savion's partner." Gah. Even just saying it sounded wrong.

I glanced over at Rory. He stared straight ahead, tapping a pencil on the desk, clearly annoyed with the situation.

I wanted to crawl in a hole and die. This was so not how having a boyfriend was supposed to go.

Mr Davis scanned the room at all the pairs of desks pushed together.

"You are now," he said. "Don't make me tell you to get to work again."

I tried to show how sorry I was to Rory, but he still wouldn't look at me.

"I guess we're partners," I said, standing next to Savion's desk.

"Guess so," he replied, but kept his eyes on the assignment sheet.

He sounded as thrilled about the arrangement as I was.

I sighed and pulled up a chair. For the rest of the period, I asked him questions about the project, and he gave me one-word answers. I don't think he ever looked up at me.

Talk about awkward.

If only that was as awkward as it got.

But no.

The bell rang, and while we were putting away our desks and chairs, Rory headed over toward me. I hoped he was ready to talk. For some reason, Savion decided to get cute.

"So, you're coming to my place tonight, right?" Savion asked me. He glanced at Rory.

"Uh— What?"

This was the break I'd been hoping for, and all I could think about was Rory.

Rory stopped in his tracks.

"To finish the project," Savion said.

Rory's shoulders sagged. He whirled on one heel and headed for the door.

"Rory, wait!" I called after him. There were a dozen kids between us.

If I hurried, I could push through them and get to Rory before he disappeared into the crowded hall.

Savion caught my arm. "We need to get going."

"I don't give a rat's ass about the project, Savion."

With the room nearly cleared out, the history teacher heard me all too clearly.

"Need I remind you it's due tomorrow?" Mr Davis said. "And after that eloquent speech, if you ditch your partner, Ms Caldwell, you'll get a zero."

Savion threw his backpack over his shoulder. Mr Davis didn't stick around for a debate. He went about tidying up his classroom.

"Fine," I said. "Let's get this over with."

If I was lucky, maybe I could get to Savion's house, let the Council in, and still meet up with Rory. Yeah. That was perfectly doable.

Savion nodded. And just like that, I had my chance to get inside the home of the sorcerer.

I had no idea my luck had just run out.

CHAPTER ELEVEN

When I imagined the place where Savion lived, I pictured a cramped basement apartment or a tiny two-bedroom house with heavy, dark drapes and skulls for decoration. Rooms that smelled of smoke and death. Fat candles dripping fat blobs of wax. Old tomes and texts in piles on dark rugs. You know, the kind of place where black magic was conjured.

The last place I expected Savion to live was a pretty rose-covered cottage with a white picket fence around a big yard filled with the snow-covered remains of gardens gone dead for the winter. It was charming, quaint, light-filled. It was all things that were the opposite of a place where black magic was conjured. And the inside was just as contrary.

The big wooden door opened to a foyer filled with light. A small table held a vase of brightly coloured flowers that gave off a light, fresh scent. A grand staircase spiralled up to the second floor. The room to our left was just as light, and the rose petal pink chairs by the fireplace, where a fire crackled, just begged to be sat in. Somewhere toward the back of the house was the kitchen, which was radiating the sweet smell of homemade chocolate chip cookies. I inhaled and sighed.

"You have such a nice house," I said, my voice filled with dreams of lovely times being had here by a loving family. I could almost see a Dalmatian tripping down the hallway chasing after a toy ball, a toddler hot on his heels. Laughter would easily fill this home. But it didn't. The harder I tried to see a happy home, the flatter the dream fell. This place was hollow.

Savion mumbled something I couldn't hear. He hung his coat on the coat stand, and tucked his boots below. I did the same.

He slung his backpack over his shoulder and asked me if I wanted anything, but he seemed uncomfortable, as if he was only asking because he thought he should, and not because he wanted to. His voice was dull and almost a whisper, and his eyes darted to the stairs like he wanted to escape to the roof.

The upstairs hallway seemed to be filled with sunshine, lit by bright lights since the sun had set as we walked here. Framed photos of a happy family that included a young Savion filled the sunny walls. A cheery rug lined the wooden floor. A vase of carnations sat on a small pedestal table. Though the flowers were fresh and the colours bright, the upper level also had that same lack of substance feeling.

His bedroom had to be close to the size of my whole apartment. Wires from game consoles to controllers crisscrossed the floor between the TV cabinet and the couch, here by the door. The bed was across the room in front of a bow window.

Savion flopped down on the chesterfield, putting aside a laptop and pushing cushions onto the floor. "Let's just get our rough drafts started, and then we can play some games." He pulled out his binder and flipped it open to the project sheet.

I took a seat on the chesterfield and reached to pull my books out of my backpack. Since walking through the front door, I'd been trying to work a few things out: what kind of person Savion really was, how his father got involved in black magic, and which object was the focus. I wondered if I should call for Ethelwulf now. At least he would have a better idea of what to look for than I.

"You have a really nice house," I said, trying to fill the awkward pause.

He paused in his writing. "Yeah. I guess."

"I'm guessing your dad's not home much?"

"Are you here to work or are you here to analyze my life?" he snapped.

I answered with a nod, and fished around in my bag for a pen. My fingers brushed against Paul's box. I heard a muffled, "Oof!" and had to cover it with a cough. I'd forgotten about him. I hoped he kept his word and stayed quiet.

Covertly, I pulled back my sleeve. The dot was still there.

Why wasn't this working?

Maybe the dots wouldn't go away until the Council arrived. But here I was inside the house, just as promised. Only I didn't have a clue what to do now.

The doorbell rang, and I practically sighed with relief. That had to be them.

Savion went downstairs to answer it, while I shoved my stuff into my backpack, and then followed.

"Where is she?" a voice demanded. "I know she came here with you."

Oh, crap.

"Rory? What are you doing here?" I took the last couple of steps slowly and came to a stop in the foyer.

Savion dipped his eyebrows, and with a smirk, he headed into the kitchen.

"Did you follow me here?" I asked.

Rory stood on the porch. The door hung wide open.

"So you really are working with him?" he asked.

"I didn't get a choice, remember?"

"But you didn't fight it that hard, either."

That's what this was about? He wanted me to fight for him?

"And," he continued, "after you spent lunch with him, I started to wonder."

"There's nothing to wonder," I said. "It's one assignment."

He nodded. "I get that."

With his arms crossed and his jaw tight, his body language said he didn't.

"But?"

He shrugged. "It's like you're not telling me everything."

"There's nothing else to tell. We got stuck doing a history assignment together. That's all."

He shook his head. "Just forget it." He turned to go.

"Rory," I called out. I wondered if he could sense Savion and I were almost-turners. For a moment, I nearly told him. But then what? I would get in trouble for telling a human about us, and Rory would only feel more alienated, more suspicious.

I finally decided to say, "I'll call you when I get home."

He waved and headed for the sidewalk. I closed the door and went to find Savion in the kitchen. He handed me a plate with a couple slices of pizza and a pile of Caesar salad.

"Thanks." I picked up a ruffle-edged slice that was loaded with pepperoni and green pepper. I sniffed garlic and oregano tomato sauce. Steam wafted off melted mozzarella cheese.

"Oh, wow," I said around a hot but delicious mouthful. I couldn't remember the last time I'd had pizza. Gran specialized in boiled potatoes with some kind of meat and vegetables from the freezer or from a can. Take-out was never an option.

I swallowed another bite and reached for one of the two cans of pop Savion had pulled from the fridge.

He was really just a normal kid. He didn't deserve to be treated the way other kids treated him. Maybe he'd been babied too much by his mom, I didn't know, but I saw a smart, nice, friendly kid, who worked hard, and who shouldn't be treated badly. So what was everyone's problem? So what if he was a little awkward. Weren't we all?

When we returned to his room and he offered me a game controller, I knew I should have refused it and gotten to work like I told Rory we were doing, but I took it. So what if the other kids didn't like him. So what if our parents were enemies. That didn't mean we couldn't be friends.

"How do you feel about music?" he asked.

"I like it," I said cautiously. Were there people who didn't?

"Good," he said, smiling. Then he got out a game that required us to use fake guitars like controllers to make music. It required a lot more coordination than I had, but it turned out to be a lot of fun. Rory would love this game.

By around song five, I finally figured out how to play, and nailed ninety percent of the song. That's when it happened. The song ended and I was so excited. I squealed and reached out to Savion for a high five. Our hands hit. A clap of thunder crashed the air. The shock of it reverberated down my arm.

I frowned.

"What's wrong?" Savion asked.

"Didn't you feel that?" I asked, though his expression made it obvious he didn't.

Then the strangest thing happened. He started to glow. It was as if someone had etched his silhouette in neon yellow and green. I wondered what the hell was wrong with him, and if it wasn't him, then it was me. Maybe I was having a seizure. Didn't people having seizures see auras? Or maybe it was migraines.

Then I remembered my conversation with Ethelwulf:

How will I know when I've found the focus?

You'll know.

No freaking way. It couldn't be— because if it was— holy crap on toast.

Savion was his father's focus.

CHAPTER TWELVE

SAVION WAS AWFULLY skinny, given how well he ate every day— and the portion sizes! Hell, the waistband of my jeans was ready to burst after just one meal here. Savion's energy had to be going somewhere. And Ethelwulf said a focus channels energy, centres it. Like a funnel.

Holy freaking crap.

Ethelwulf was right. When I found it, I would know it. Savion was his father's focus. I knew it all the way down to my toes.

"Are you okay?" he asked, reaching out to put a hand on my shoulder. I backed away. I couldn't let him touch me again. Once had changed everything. No telling what would happen a second time.

"Actually, I have a headache," I said and held my hand to my forehead for effect and so he couldn't see the lie in my eyes.

He nodded. "I'll turn the volume down," he said and he did.

"I should probably get going anyway." I shoved my books into my bag. Now that I knew what the focus was, I had to find a way to contact Ethelwulf. He'd said all I had to do was call his name, but it couldn't be that simple, could it?

I hoped so. Because my summoning spells sucked dishwater.

"Oh." Was it just me or was there disappointment in his voice?

Downstairs, a door closed with a loud bang.

"My father's home," Savion said, going to his door. "Can you stay long enough to meet him?"

"Er—" Did I really want to meet him now that I knew what he was doing to his son? And what would happen when we were introduced? Wouldn't he know by my name that I was my mother's daughter? History project or not, he would figure out this was not coincidence.

I'd told Ethelwulf this mission would have problems.

"You look really pale," he said. "I'll get my dad to check you over. He's a doctor."

"He's a—" I think my eyeballs just about launched into space.

"Doctor."

I couldn't breathe. "I really have to get going."

"I insist. You look like you're about to collapse." He made like he was going to 'help' me to the chesterfield.

I flopped down and held my backpack in front of me like a shield before he could touch me again. Okay, where was the back door? How far down was the drop from the window? What was my best chance to get out of here right now?

"Stay," he commanded. "I'll be right back."

As soon as I heard his feet on the stairs, I opened my bag.

"Paul, it's Savion," I whispered. "I don't have much time. You gotta help me."

"You're Melantha, not Savion. What are you trying to pull?" Paul said back. He sounded kind of grumpy.

"Focus."

"I am focused. He's right. You do need to see a doctor. There is something seriously wrong with you."

"Savion is the focus."

He laughed. "Did you hit your head?"

I didn't laugh. My chin started to quiver. I bit my lip so I wouldn't start crying.

Then Paul put it together. "Are you sure?"

"There was a clap of thunder and then Savion started to glow."

"Mother Mabel's mustard molasses," he swore.

"What do I do?"

"How should I know?"

"He's gone to get his father to meet me."

"Oh, crapsicles. You gotta get out of here."

"Help me!"

"Maybe my jumping skills will amaze him to death. I got nothing!"

"I thought you were here to help me!"

"I'm here for advice, sweetcakes."

"And?"

"And I advise you to get the hell out of here!"

I took a deep breath and tried to not crush him like the bug he was.

I tried again. "Ethelwulf said once I found the focus, the Council would find me. How does that work?"

"What makes you think I should know?"

I heard footsteps on the stairs. "They're coming."

"No crap, Sherlock!"

Frustrated, I zipped the bag shut. And I wasn't gentle about it. Stupid, cricket.

"Ow!" Paul's cry was muffled by the books.

"Shhh!" Where the hell was Ethelwulf?

Savion and his father walked in.

"Father," Savion said formally, "I'd like you to meet Mel. We're working on a history project together. Mel, this is my father."

"Nice to meet you," I said. I started to rise and reach out to shake his hand, but he put one hand on my shoulder and pulled out a penlight in the other.

"Just a minute," he said, shining the light in my eyes. "Savion says you are not feeling well." He jammed his fingertips under my jawbone. "I don't think it's anything serious."

He gripped my chin, turning my face to examine both my cheeks. "You do look unusually pale, though. Perhaps you need to eat more iron."

"Thank you, sir. I should be heading home. My Gran will take care of me there," I said faintly. My heartbeat was running like the Calgary Stampede.

He smiled, breaking up the concern on his face. He was a lot like Savion, but older, more muscular. If I didn't already know who he was and what he'd done, I might trust him with my life. Completely. He had such a trusting kind of face.

"You don't need to call me sir. You are a friend of my son. You call me Gerrard, okay?"

I nodded, swallowing.

He started to turn away, but then paused, peering at me in a way I didn't like.

"Do I—? Have we met?" he asked.

Crap. Did he recognize my mother in me?

I shook my head. "I don't think so." I glanced at Savion, but he was picking up empty pop cans.

Gerrard was still peering at me, and it was totally creeping me out.

"Maybe it was at the hospital," I suggested.

He shrugged. "Maybe. But I work in cancer research now."

Gerrard nodded. "Not long now, my son. Soon I will have a cure and then all that we have sacrificed will have been worth it."

There was something about what he just said that made my skin crawl. And he'd seemed like such a nice man up until now.

I picked up my backpack, and was about to beg my leave and go home, when Gerrard's wristwatch began to glow a bright green that matched the unsettling colours still hovering around Savion. Gerrard glanced at his wrist. His face clouded over, his eyes narrowed, he let out a growl.

The doorbell rang. That's pretty much when all hell broke loose.

***

I'd never been in a war before, let alone caught at the heart of one, but that's exactly where I found myself. Gerrard took me by the arm and dragged me down the stairs. I scrambled to keep my feet under me. Savion and his protests trailed behind us.

"Savion! Your guest said she has to be going! You will see her to the door!" He released me in the foyer, pushing me toward the door.

"But father— what's wrong?"

The doorbell continued to ring.

"Everything, Savion! They will destroy everything!"

"Who are they?"

Gerrard took Savion by the shoulders. "These people, they want to destroy everything. I cannot let that happen." He gave him a quick hug and then headed for the kitchen.

"Father, your watch—" Savion said, watching him go.

"There's not time!" he called from the kitchen.

I stared at the front door. Someone was pounding so hard it hurt my ears. Was there a battering ram out there? I turned back at Savion to see if he was going to answer it, but he was gone.

The pounding ceased for a moment and I heard Paul's muffled voice come from my bag. I couldn't understand what he was saying. I guessed there was no harm in getting him out now. Things were weird enough.

"I'd step back if I were you!" he shouted as soon as I had his box in my hand.

"Why?" Then I heard the crack of splitting wood. Another boom, and the heavy door separated from the frame at the hinges. I scooted out of the way just as what was left of the door crashed to the tiled floor. I landed on my butt, looking up to see a tall, nasty creature in the doorway. An ogre.

The ogre pulled back his blue-green lips and bared sharp yellow teeth in an angry sneer and growled.

"Er, hello." It sounded like Ethelwulf's voice, coming from somewhere behind the creature. An elbow wedged between the ogre and the door frame, and then Ethelwulf's head pushed through the hole.

"This is Thorn," the elf said to me, then turned his head to address the creature. "Now step back and let me talk to her."

The ogre grunted, but he stepped back, watching me with narrowed eyes and his bulky arms folded across his chest.

Ethelwulf took the ogre's place on the doorstep. The cold wind circled around on the floor. Cold came up off the floor tiles through my jeans so I stood up. The elf dusted off his suit, straightened his jacket and cleared his throat as though he expected something.

"They went to the kitchen," I said. "Maybe there's a door to the basement there."

I expected them to go running after Gerrard. Why were they standing there looking expectantly at me?

"Is she going to let us in or what? It's cold out here," said a squeaky voice from behind the ogre.

"How many of you are there?" I asked.

"Enough," the elf answered. "But the black magic sorcerer has this place well-guarded. You have to invite us in."

I opened my mouth to extend the invitation, when I remembered. "Wait. There's a problem."

"I'm sure whatever it is, we'll work it out, but you must let us in before he gets a chance to build defenses and escape."

"I want you to promise you won't hurt Savion."

"The boy? Why on earth would we hurt him? He hasn't the powers for black magic yet."

Ethelwulf was good at dodging the issue, but now was not the time for it.

"Just promise," I said.

He sighed. "All right. I promise we won't hurt him. Now will you let us in?"

"You may come in," I said and they did. All eight of them. First Ethelwulf and then Thorn, three identical men in identical top hats, a shriveled up old woman with long white hair, and a young woman with short pink hair, who was holding a rope that was attached at the other end to a goat. With the exception of the ogre and the goat, they all carried shiny black canes. Council members.

"What's the goat for?" I asked, wrinkling my nose at the strong barnyard smell.

"You don't want to know," Paul said from the box still in my hand.

"Now, Melantha, tell us where the focus is," Ethelwulf said.

"It's Savion," I said, regretting it the moment it came out of my mouth and they all gasped.

Then I remembered: they were going to pull the sorcerer's spells out of him.

"Remember, you promised," I said, feeling desperate.

Ethelwulf's face didn't change.

"Paul, please go with Melantha to our transport outside." He turned and nodded at Thorn. The ogre and the top hats headed for the kitchen. Then he addressed the women and the goat. "It's as we feared—"

"Wait," I interjected. "You knew it was Savion?"

"We suspected as much. Just look at the poor boy. Funnelling power through him has syphoned his own natural instincts. His lack of courage is a dead giveaway."

My idea of courage must be different from Ethelwulf's, but I had more important things to argue about at that moment.

"So you just used me to get in here."

He blinked. "The lab is downstairs. We need to get in there—"

"You said you needed the focus. You lied to me. You used me."

"We will still—" He was cut off by a great crash. It sounded like a truck smashed into the house. A low rumble shook the floor.

"Earthquake," I said.

Ethelwulf's voice was clear and serious. "No."

He stared in the direction of the kitchen. He motioned for the ladies and the goat to follow him.

"I fear we may be too late," he said.

"Wait— what are you going to do?" I asked. I started to panic as I thought of my role in Savion's fate. What kind of friend was I?

"We will do what we must," he replied as he marched on, sounding like a battle-weary soldier recruited out of retirement. "You will wait in the van."

Wait in the van? No way. But even as I knew I didn't want to, I also knew he was probably right. He was a wise old elf and everything he'd told me had been true so far— well, except for the lie about how long I'd had to make my decision, and the lie about how they didn't know Savion was the focus. But he'd admitted he'd lied to work around Gran. If anyone understood the need to lie to work around Gran, it was me.

And I suspected he didn't mention Savion was the focus because he didn't want to scare me off. Logic should have told me Savion was the focus. I mean, what else would a man kill for, if not his own family? Even so, Ethelwulf should have said something. Even his suspicions. Maybe he didn't trust me. Maybe he didn't have a reason to trust me. I hadn't come into my powers yet. I wasn't strong enough to get involved in this.

I wondered if I didn't have to get involved to be of help. Maybe I could get Savion to the van, too. It could work.

Then I remembered his father would be drawing his powers through his son. Did want to witness that?

Did I want a hole in my head??

I headed for the van. I actually wanted to live long enough to do stuff someday.

I scooped up my backpack and reached the open doorway when three things happened that made everything change. One: there was another crash, a sort of screech on screech that sounded like train cars slamming into each other, and it was followed by a rumbling and rattling of the floors, walls and windows. Two: a high-pitched primal cry of pain reached out and drew shivers down my spine and I knew I'd only moments ago seen the face of the very being who was suffering that much pain. And three: as I stood there frozen by the scream that stopped as suddenly as it began, the tremors died away, and the coat rack fell to the floor, a silence fell over the house that was more than just silence, it was a void, an emptiness that had consumed the life and light of everything that had once lived here.

The silence was filled by Paul's one-word whisper, "Ethelwulf."

CHAPTER THIRTEEN

I FELT LIKE my stomach had dropped through the floor. He couldn't mean that scream came from the wise, powerful, old elf.

"No, no, no, no, no," he whimpered, and my heart broke. Tears stung in my eyes. I strained to hear some sign— any sign— that Ethelwulf was okay. Even a scream. Anything but that horrible silence.

We couldn't lose him. He was our best chance to capture my mother's killer, to save Savion.

"Are you sure?" I asked.

Paul didn't answer, so I asked again.

"I've heard him like that only once before," he finally said. "It was a battle long ago. Many lives were lost that day."

The silence ended with the sound of soft booms, like thunder on the horizon. My feet were held in place, shackled by my own fear. I wanted to know what was happening. I wanted to know if Ethelwulf was okay.

I didn't see how I could wait outside now. Even the icy wind blew through my jeans and sweatshirt, begging me to seek shelter. How could I turn my back on people I cared about while they were caught in a life or death situation?

I went to the kitchen and found the door to the basement. The booming grew louder when I pulled it open.

"What do you think you're doing?" Paul snapped from inside his box.

"I can't stand it anymore, Paul," I confessed. "I have to help them."

"You? What are you going to do but get in the way?" It sounded like he was trying to scold me, but there was no snort, no derision. It was only a half-hearted attempted, probably because he wanted to be down there, too.

"I don't know. But I know I have to try. Are you going to stop me?"

He snorted. "Like anything can stop you once you've made up your mind. I've seen you in action."

I felt relieved. That sounded more like Paul. "Good. So we're agreed."

"Wait— If we're doing this, then we're going in low. Stay quiet, stay to the shadows, stay out of sight." He hung upside down at the top of the box, clinging to the mesh. He turned his head at an odd angle so he could see out.

"Really."

He ignored my sarcasm. "When I say it's time to get out of there, you get the hell out of there, but you wait for my signal."

"Signal?" It seemed to me he was enjoying this.

"You'll know it when you hear it. We're going down for a peek, there's nothing much else you can do, anyway, but if we get caught, I will disavow all knowledge of your actions."

"Disavow?" I rolled my eyes. "You'll be with me. How do you figure you can 'disavow all knowledge of my actions'?" He was definitely enjoying himself.

"I'll just tell them I was sleeping," he said.

"Are you done now?"

"We move on my signal. Ready?" The booming sounds seemed to be moving farther away from us. "Now!"

I shook my head as I placed one foot on the top step. It creaked as I lowered my full weight onto it.

Paul let out a loud, "Shhhhh!"

"You 'shhh'!" I whispered. "You're louder than the stairs."

"Hmph." He dropped into the box, turned his back on me and curled up in the corner, glaring just before he turned his face away.

I shook my head. A cricket that was a drama queen. I'd never have believed it if I hadn't seen it with my own eyes.

The staircase was steep, like the basement stairs in the house I grew up in. A shelf ran along where the main floor jutted into the space for the stairs. In our house, the stairwell was unfinished, as was the basement, but this stairwell was clean, finished, the shelf filled with baskets of cheerful silk flowers, and the stairs covered in beige carpet. It should have felt cozy and welcoming, but as I descended, I felt even more afraid than I ever did descending into the dark, dismal basement at my old house.

Lights were on in the basement. The furnished rooms should have felt bright and cheery. In some areas the lights had been smashed out; burn marks marred the ceiling, and they smelled fresh. Maybe at one time these had been friendly rooms, but now they were choked with heavy emotion, like swimming in pools of thick, black oil. The feeling was in complete contrast to the bright flowery upholstery, the white wooden furniture, and the sunny yellow walls. I should have felt warm, cozy and welcome. Instead, I was scared stiff.

I stopped at the bottom of the stairs feeling like a child confronting the monsters behind the furnace. I wondered how the others had coped with coming down here. All I knew was the feeling I had was because of a spell. There had to be a way to beat it.

"Hey," Paul called out. "What are you waiting for?"

I stood on that last step, taking in a room that spread out to my left, a room with a TV inside a wardrobe, couches and chairs and a gas fireplace with a glowing flame flickering behind the glass. In front of me and to my right were closed doors. At the other end of the family room, opposite the direction of the stairs, was another door, and it was open. I stuck my head around the wall and tried to see through the open doorway. It was dark back there. Dark, but lit occasionally with flashes of bright light that coincided with the booms. It seemed to be the place to go, but I couldn't quite make my feet go there.

"I can't do it," I whispered. I climbed up a step.

"Well, sure you can. You just sneak over and take a peek," Paul explained logically. "Just a peek so we can see if— uh— if everyone is all right."

There was nothing logical about telling a kid to go climb into the witch's hot oven.

"Forget it," I said, backing up two more steps.

"But we're practically there!"

"I know."

"So why in Merlin's name are you getting cold feet now?" He drew in a breath. "Oh, I get it. It's guarded, isn't it?"

I backed up another step. I had no idea if it was guarded or not, but it seemed as logical explanation as any. Why else wouldn't I be able to enter the room?

"Okay," Paul said. "Here's what you're going to do: take a deep breath, think happy thoughts, and run. It's not that far. You can make it."

"Think happy thoughts? You really think that will work?" This guard wasn't like the invisible barrier Ethelwulf had put up back at the apartment when he didn't want me to leave the room. This guard was filthy. It was like being dragged through a sticky tar pit of negative emotions. Where Ethelwulf's barrier physically repelled me, the sorcerer's guard was turning my own mind against me.

"Sure. Why not?" Paul said. But it sounded like even he was just guessing.

I wanted to help Ethelwulf, I really did, but I didn't believe Paul's plan would work. It couldn't be that simple to bypass powerful magic. Still, he continued to insist, and he was the expert, so I took a deep breath, thought about the winter nights I'd spent watching movies with my mom and dad, and ran. I got to the bottom of the stairs, felt like I'd been attacked by a roomful of creepy crawly bugs, and turned around and ran up the stairs.

"Wait!" Paul cried. "You're going the wrong way!"

"I don't care," I answered, taking the stairs two at a time. I pushed the door shut behind me, but I didn't feel comfortable with the basement at my back, so I wheeled around and backed up until I came up against the cabinets. I shuddered, but the horrible feeling lingered, sticking like clusters of burrs on my clothing that wouldn't brush off no matter how hard I tried.

"What are you doing? Why are we back up here?" Paul asked, standing up on his hind legs. He grasped the wire with his front legs. His antennae poked up through the wire mesh and twitched, tasting the air.

"I can't do it," I said, between panting breaths. My heart raced, blood pounded in my ears.

"Oh, well. I guess I can't blame you. I was never able to get past a good guard spell, either."

"What are you talking about? You're just a cricket."

"What do you think I was before I was a cricket?"

"A mouse?" I guessed.

"True, but before that I was a wizard."

"You mean spell-turner."

"I mean wizard."

"What's the difference?"

"Wait. Do you hear that?"

"What?"

"Something's changed."

I was about to ask what he meant, but I was interrupted by a boom that rocked the house. The force of the blast knocked me off balance and pushed me to the floor. Paul's box fell out of my hands as I reached for something to hold onto. Then everything went still and silent. Just as I struggled to get back to my feet and find Paul's box, I became aware of footsteps thundering up the stairs.

The door opened and Gerrard burst out, towing Savion behind him. The fingers of his left hand squeezed around Savion's skinny bicep in a grip so tight Gerrard's knuckles were white and the marks on his son's skin were angry red.

"Run, Mel!" Paul shouted. But I barely heard him over the shock of seeing Savion.

Savion bled from a slash across his forehead. He shivered, wearing only a t-shirt in the house made cold by the broken front door. His skin was paler than usual. Judging by the hollow expression on his face, and the way his limbs hung like limp dish rags, his father's grip was the only thing holding him up.

"Use the Council's powers!" Paul cried. "Mel, capture him!"

Gerrard saw me then, standing in his kitchen.

"Back off, you bully!" Paul shouted. "You want Mel? You'll have to deal with me first!"

Gerrard kicked Paul's box and it went sailing across the kitchen. Before I could move, Gerrard grabbed the front of my shirt and hauled me to my feet. His hair was dishevelled, in crazy clumps. A streak of blood was smeared across his face. His eyes were veiled in dark shadows.

"You," he seethed. "You brought them here. You've cost me everything."

I don't know what he intended to do with me. I didn't think it would be very nice. I had to do something.

From the moment Gerrard touched me, I felt power itching in my fingertips. At first it was a mild buzzing as though I had my hands on an electric razor. I'd tried to ignore it. But it had swelled to pins and needles, throbbing in my fingers like they were asleep, refusing to be ignored. I let the power swirl onto my palms like snow across an icy sidewalk and then — not knowing what else to do with it— I put my hands to his chest and set it free.

He let go of me and stumbled back as if I'd just hit him with a wrecking ball. His free arm flailed as he wobbled back, trying not to fall on his son. For a moment, I thought it had worked.

"You—! You—!" he screamed. "I'll get you."

The transfer of power left me feeling hollow and weak. My knees buckled under me and I slumped to the floor. While he regained control of his feet and momentum, all I could do was watch as he descended upon me.

His eyes burned dark with anger. His mouth hardly opened when he spoke, but when he did, he showed teeth clenched tight. His voice was low, deep and terrifying.

"I enjoyed draining the magic out of your nosey mother. She should have stayed out of my business. I'm trying to save us all and she had to ruin it!" He grabbed my arm and hauled me up, putting his face into mine.

"I wonder," he murmured, "will you scream the way she did? Will you beg for mercy like she did?"

Right then and there I knew he would not let me live. He would make me suffer for everything he believed she and I had cost him.

His fingernails dug into my flesh and I wished that was all that happened, because I could have dealt with that, but he didn't stop, and somehow I knew he wasn't capable of stopping. He would never stop. There would never be enough power for him. Death meant nothing to him. He only wanted life. And at that moment he wanted my life.

His fingernails pierced my skin, causing blood to swell to the surface and pain to rush through my entire body, flaring with the intensity of magnesium on fire. I screamed. White hot sparks ran through my veins, streaming to Gerrard's fingers as if they were answering his call. In a matter of only seconds, my vision blurred with coloured dots, and my body went weak.

Savion's voice floated like a beacon from the fog, weak at first, but growing louder.

"Father," he said. It may not have been the first time he said it. "Father, please. Don't do this. Don't hurt her anymore."

Gerrard didn't respond to his son's pleas.

"Please, father. Leave her. We must go now. They are coming."

Gerrard faltered. His grip lessened, though he did not release my arm, the intensity of the energy harvest was interrupted. I fell, weak and drained. He lost his grip, and once again, I hit the floor.

"Savion? Son?"

"I am here, father. Hurry. We must leave."

"They are coming?"

"Yes, father."

"I can stop them now, son. I have her blood. I have her power. My strength returns. I can save us. Save us all."

"No, father. Not now. Now, I must rest."

"Rest..."

"Please, father. Take me where I can rest. Take me to our summer home. They won't find us there. You can rest."

"Yes, my son. We will rest. Then I shall return."

CHAPTER FOURTEEN

THE PINK-HAIRED spell-turner found me first. She was there when I opened my eyes, though I didn't remember closing them. I wanted two things. One, to know what she was doing in my bedroom, and two, a glass of water with a side dish of pain killers. My brain pounded against my skull like a cannon fire. I wanted nothing more than to hide under the covers, to be warm. But there were no covers. There was only pain.

"Where—" I tried to say, but couldn't remember what I was asking. Then the memories of my evening at Savion's came rushing back.

"Can you hear me?" she asked. She appeared to be no more than a few years older than me, though odds were good she was a great deal older. Magic could hide a user's age.

"Savion," I said, despite my scratchy throat. "We have to go after him."

"We don't know where they went."

"But they said— their summer home."

"Okay."

I swallowed against the burning in my throat. Emotion overwhelmed the pain. "Eth—"

"You can see him soon. Do you think you can sit up?"

I didn't know her for more than a few minutes, but I sensed she wasn't exactly being completely honest. The old woman was more helpful. She appeared behind the pink-haired girl.

"You can't tell her that!" the old woman gasped. She'd lowered the hood of her coat, and her white hair fell down almost to her waist.

The pink-haired girl turned her head slightly to the other turner. Through tight lips, she said, "Yes, I can. I thought you were with him."

The old woman shrugged. "The Three Ps are with him. They know elves better than I."

The girl sighed. "Could you get a glass of water, please?"

The younger turner had a pixie-ish face, softened by her mild manner and concern for my welfare. Her blue eyes, however, seemed to carry the weight of the world and were red and puffy as if she'd been crying.

"I'm Rhiannon," she said. "Do you think you can sit up?"

I nodded and lifted my arm. She braced her arm under me and helped me sit with my back against the Lebrun's kitchen cabinets.

"This is Horatia," she said, accepting the glass of water from the old woman. She held the glass to my mouth so I could take a sip.

"I'm Mel—" I started to say after I swallowed.

"Melantha Caldwell. We know. I'm sorry we didn't meet under better circumstances."

She placed the back of her small hand to my forehead.

I brushed her hand away. "What are you doing?"

She smiled, showing small teeth, with slightly pointed canines. Maybe she thought the smile would make me feel more comfortable. It didn't. Probably because she seemed nervous.

"Just checking," she explained helpfully. "Do you remember what happened to you?"

I told her what I remembered of Gerrard and how he sucked hot sparks from my blood.

"He drained my magic," I said.

She nodded. She didn't seem happy to hear it, but she didn't look like she believed me, either.

"I'm serious," I said. "Gerrard has found a way to drain the magic out of turners."

"Why would he do that?"

"I don't know, but once he did, it was like he was drunk off my power. He was incoherent and stuff."

The old woman was more help, again.

"Horrors!" the woman gasped. "It couldn't be worse."

"What?" I asked, wondering if I should work up the energy to panic. My body, especially my eyelids, felt like I was made with wet cement.

"Horatia," Rhiannon said, giving her a stern look.

"But the girl must be told! Her power—"

"Not now. Our priority at the moment is to get Ethelwulf—" She cut herself off, glancing at me. "We have other priorities, Horatia," she said simply, though her eyes pleaded with the other woman.

Horatia sniffed, tilting her chin. "I shall see if the elves need me. I trust you'll be along shortly?" She didn't wait for an answer. The air cracked, and then the old woman was gone.

"Okay," Rhiannon said, letting out a sigh of relief. "Let's get you home."

"I can't go home."

"You've done nothing wrong here. You're not in trouble. I'll talk to Alberta. The best place for you right now is with a white turner. Alberta knows the spells to help you heal."

"She isn't there."

"I'm sure wherever she is, she'll come home to help you."

"She can't." I explained that Ethelwulf imprisoned her in a blue orb because she so strenuously objected to this mission.

As I explained, Rhiannon's pale complexion became even paler. She went very still.

"Gran's okay, isn't she? Even if Ethelwulf is hurt?" I stumbled over the last word. The alternate was unthinkable.

"Um, yeah," she said, but she studied the pattern of the floor tiles and spoke in the same voice as when she tried to cover Ethelwulf's condition.

"What do you mean 'yeah'? Is she all right or isn't she?" I demanded. This time panic rose, and I wasn't able to stop it.

"Our priority now is to get you somewhere you can rest."

"Screw your priorities! Tell me what happened to Gran!"

Anger flashed behind her blue eyes. She probably wasn't used to having people defy her 'priorities'.

"We were all knocked out by Lebrun's blast. Ethelwulf took the hit directly. When we came to, we found him—" She licked her teeth and swallowed. "We've managed to stabilize his condition, but he remains unconscious. The Three Ps transported him to the Sanctuary. I came to check on you."

I studied her. She had more to say. "And? Did you see a blue orb?"

She lowered her gaze. "There was an orb. It rolled out of Ethelwulf's coat when he fell. I don't know what happened to it."

"Is it downstairs?"

She flexed her jaw. I thought she was about to say something, but then she shook her head.

"We have to go check," I said, trying to get up. My head swirled. Getting up wasn't a good idea, but I tried anyway.

"The basement was clear of all magic when I came up the stairs." She spoke in a soft whisper. Emotion choked her. Tears shone in her eyes.

"Maybe you missed it. It's not very big."

"I didn't. Size doesn't matter. Magic is magic."

"So he has her," I said carefully. Gerrard Lebrun had her. He'd killed my mother and now he had my Gran.

She nodded. Neither of us said anything for a while.

"So what happens now?" I asked after the silence seemed to go on too long.

"I'll have to take you to the Sanctuary. You're not safe here alone."

"I've never been there. What is it?"

She smiled. "It's the place where turners go to get away from the world." Her smile was short-lived. "Let's get out of here. This place gives me the creeps."

"Where will we go when get there?" I asked, with her cane in one hand, she offered me her other hand and helped me to my feet. I was feeling a little stronger, though still shaky. I felt less like I'd been hit by a truck and more like I had the flu.

"My place," she said simply.

"But where is this Sanctuary? How do we get there?" Maybe I wasn't doing as well as I thought. I was getting a headache trying to figure out what she was saying.

She smiled patiently. "The Sanctuary is connected to everyone who needs it. It's not attached to one specific place."

I still didn't get it. She continued, "I'll explain more when we get there. Right now, I'd really like to get out of here."

"Sure," I said, but I wasn't feeling it. I had more questions than I knew what to do with. I grabbed my backpack and reached for Paul's box. Then I remembered that I'd dropped it. And then I realized it had been quite a while since Paul had made a sound.

A hot flare of worry shot up my spine.

"Paul?" I almost couldn't say his name. He could be hurt or worse. And it was my fault. I'd dropped the box. I should have been more careful. And I should have realized I hadn't heard from him in a while; I should have started searching for him sooner.

I found the box on its side under the kitchen table. The lid was open.

"Paul?" I started crawling on the floor, almost frantically, and had to stop myself. I had to be careful. What if I crushed Paul while I searched for him?

"Who are you looking for?" Rhiannon asked, crouching by the table.

"Paul," I said, trying not to cry. "The cricket. Ethelwulf gave him to me."

"Paulinus?" she asked, sounding surprised. No, more like shocked.

"Paul. The cricket. Oh, where is he?" Panic rose again, hot with worry for Ethelwulf and Gran, and in my weakened state, I started to tremble. "Paul?"

"Over here," came a small croak. I went in the direction of his voice, and found him under the vertical blinds in front of the sliding patio doors.

"Paul!" I reached to pick him up.

"Whoa! Be careful!" he said, and then I saw the reason and I understood why he'd been so quiet.

"Oh, no," I moaned. He cried out as I carefully lifted him and placed him onto my hand. His rear leg on his right side was bent in a way it was never meant to be bent.

"Just leave me," he moaned. "I'm nothing more than a cat toy now."

"I'm not leaving you here." I turned to Rhiannon. "Someone at the Sanctuary will help him, right?"

She snorted. "Paulinus Gennarus Magnus the Third? I think not."

"Don't call me that. I've not been that name since— It's Paul now. Not that it matters, since I'm dying."

"You're not dying," I said, wishing he wouldn't say such things. "You have a broken leg." I felt relieved to see he was feeling well enough to be dramatic. I didn't know what the problem was between him and Rhiannon.

She snorted again. "Leave him. We must go."

"I'm not just leaving him here!"

"He's not coming with you to the Sanctuary. I won't be seen with him! You come alone or you don't come at all."

"What have you done?" I asked Paul. I probably should have known to ask him before now.

"It's a long story. I'm sure everyone's forgotten about it," he croaked. "You should leave me to die than let me suffer another moment with her."

Rhiannon pursed her lips and crossed her arms over her chest.

"Out with it," I said, "because I have nowhere to go, and I don't know what's happened to Gran or Ethelwulf, and someone still has to save Savion, I desperately need to sleep, and now I can't feel my toes!"

I got to the end of all that and nearly burst into tears. I held it back, but my chin quivered and tears welled up in my eyes. I sniffed.

Paul spoke first. He addressed Rhiannon. "Won't you make an exception?" he asked. "It was a long time ago. I've done so much good since then."

"I'm already taking a risk bringing in this almost-turner," she responded, but now with less venom.

"Stop quoting Star Wars, Paul," I interjected. "Start being sincere."

"Couldn't you do it for Ethelwulf? He charged me with keeping an eye on her. You wouldn't want to be the one who keeps me from doing my job, would you?"

She sighed. "Fine. But I'll crush you under my boot before I let anyone find out you're with me."

Whoa. He must have really ticked off a bunch of people. I couldn't wait to hear this story.

"You're a good person, Rhiannon," he said solemnly. I placed him in his box. With my free hand I slung my bag over my shoulder and then took Rhiannon's waiting hand.

"Ready?" she asked.

"Ready." I answered, and with a tap of her shiny black cane, the air cracked, and time and space split open, sucking me into its wide mouth. I shut my eyes as the air exploded around me. I felt torn apart and slammed back together. When I opened my eyes, I found we stood between two brick buildings in an alley that smelled like teriyaki beef and sour cabbage. Dented in one of the walls, a glossy black door with a shiny silver knob loomed above us.

"We're here," Rhiannon announced. She dropped my hand and turned the knob, opening the door to another world.

CHAPTER FIFTEEN

RHIANNON WENT THROUGH the door without hesitation, and I had no choice but to follow. We stepped out onto a really wide cobblestone street with Victorian two- and three-story brick buildings running down both sides. Shops filled the bottoms of the buildings, apartments filled the tops. Lampposts with actual flames atop them dotted the sidewalks, but there was no need to worry about where one walked for there were no cars on these streets. These were streets meant for the horse-drawn buggies parked outside these shops. At least some of the buggies were drawn by horses. Others were pulled by creatures I didn't recognize. There were spell-turners and creatures of every kind everywhere, and the shop signs indicated these were no ordinary places of business.

"This is the Sanctuary?"

"Of course," Rhiannon said.

"Wow," I gasped. "How—" I started, but Rhiannon cut me off. She strode ahead of me out of the alcove and then took a left turn onto the street.

"There will be time for that later," she said.

I shut up and let her lead me down the street. There was no snow in the Sanctuary, nor was it freezing cold, despite the clear, star-filled night sky over our heads.

I could get used to a place like this. It was the best feeling and the worst feeling. For the first time in my life, I was surrounded by people like me. I wouldn't have to hide that I wasn't human here. It was a freedom I'd never known.

But I wasn't able to share this moment with my mother or Gran or anyone I loved.

A sign hanging outside a storefront down the street caught my eye. A Matter of Focus.

"Is that—?" I started.

"Later," the pink-haired turner said over her shoulder, giving me a pointed look.

Rhiannon moved off the road, stepping up to the sidewalk outside a shop that specialized in pots and pans. Hanging in the window were copper pots just like the ones Gran preferred to stir spells in.

We didn't go into the shop; instead we went in a door next to the shop and up a narrow staircase. At the top of the stairs was a hallway of doors. Rhiannon went straight over to a white door with "214" in black metal numbers on the front. She knocked and waited. Inside, footsteps clopped on hardwood floors, and then the door opened.

"'Bout time," Horatia said, letting us into the dimly lit room. But as soon as she saw me, she half shut the door and kept us in the hallway.

"What's she doing here?" the old woman asked.

Rhiannon explained, ending with the statement "I assume full responsibility for Melantha while she's here."

Horatia narrowed her eyes. "And the box?"

Rhiannon sighed. "Paulinus."

Horatia's already pale face somehow became paler. "You're joking."

Rhiannon shook her head.

"Of all the rat-faced, stinkle thorns in all the—"

"I can hear you," Paul interjected.

"Good!" Horatia said.

"Are you going to let us in or not?" I asked. Honestly. What had Paul done? He and I were going to have a long chat.

She glanced at Rhiannon. "Are you assuming responsibility for him?"

The pink-haired turner shook her head.

"I am," I said.

Horatia raised her eyebrows at me. "Are you sure you want to do that, almost-turner?"

If I was to be honest, I was starting wonder that myself. I just wasn't sure I wanted anyone else knowing that. Not until I talked to Paul and found out what all the fuss was about. For all I knew they were mad at him because he ate the last cookie.

I nodded. "Yep. If that's going to be a problem for anyone, I can always go back home and fend for myself against the sorcerer. I'm sure Ethelwulf wouldn't mind if you all leave me in the real world defenseless against a sorcerer hopped up on my blood."

Horatia opened the door. "No, no. Now we can't have that."

Rhiannon went inside and I followed. I recognized the place right away. I'd previously viewed the room from above, inside Gran's copper pot. This was Ethelwulf's place. The dark furniture, the wardrobe, the shelves loaded with unusual objects were all just as I'd seen them before. The goat tethered to the table was a new addition.

I'm not sure what I expected to see when I gazed up at the ceiling, but all I found was a normal plaster swirl with a dusty chandelier hanging over the living room.

"Have a seat," Rhiannon said to me, though she and Horatia went straight into the room behind the closed door. From the brief glimpse I saw, it must be the elf's bedroom.

She didn't say where I should sit, but since Thorn took up most of Ethelwulf's chesterfield, I chose to sit opposite him and occupy the wooden chair next to the bedroom door. From there I could watch the goat nibble on a square bale of hay, and listen to the hushed conversation in the bedroom.

"How is he?" Rhiannon asked.

"The same," came Horatia's reply. "I've sent the Three Ps to get the Elders."

"Well, at least the alacroport didn't worsen his condition."

Horatia harrumphed a noise of agreement.

"Once the Elders arrive, we should go after Lebrun before he can restore his powers."

"How? We don't even know where he is! No one witnessed his escape."

"Melantha did. She said they're going to their summer home."

"The cottage on the Mattawa River?"

"Must be. Our research has found only that place other than his home and office. If we go now—"

"Are you out of your mind? We can't go without Ethelwulf!"

"We'll find another to be our seventh. There are—"

"No. It will take too long to complete a security clearance."

"It won't take that long, Horatia."

"It's too hard to find anyone willing to stick their neck out to stand up against black magic, Rhiannon. And once they find out who we're going after, you can bet they'll go right back to keeping their heads in the sand."

"You're right." The younger turner sounded so defeated.

"It would be better to wait for Ethelwulf," Horatia said, her voice softer, her tone more gentle than before.

"But in the time it takes for Ethelwulf to heal, Lebrun will also regain strength."

"It is a risk, yes. But one that is necessary for the entire magical community."

The knot in my stomach tightened. Ethelwulf needed time to heal. How badly was he hurt?

I didn't have time to consider the situation. The door to Ethelwulf's apartment opened, and in came an endless stream of figures in dark, hooded robes, and the Three Ps. I counted nine robed figures, and with the three elves, they all crammed into Ethelwulf's bedroom and shut the door.

As they passed, Thorn nodded at the Three Ps. Once all were behind the closed door, and the apartment empty, Thorn removed the goat's tether from the table, and pulled the animal over to the chesterfield. He opened a large burlap bag stamped "OATS" on the front. The goat thrust its head inside the bag and made voracious munching sounds.

"Good, Maxi," Thorn said, patting it on the side. "This is Maximus Hircus. He's a good goat," he said to me.

I nodded. I didn't know anything about goats. I tried to eavesdrop, but there was too much chatter going on; I couldn't make out what anyone was saying. There was nothing else to do but make small talk with the ogre.

"Can he talk, too?"

Thorn frowned. "No, he's just a goat."

"I'm sorry about earlier," I said. "I didn't mean to be startled by you when I opened the door."

I glanced at the tall grandfather clock in the corner. If it was right, if it was on the same time as back home in Ottawa, then it was currently almost three in the morning. Was it really that late? It seemed like time had flown by, but my body said it hadn't. My body said it hadn't slept properly in a week.

"Me sorry too. Friends?" He turned up his turquoise lips in a smile, and held out a scale-covered green hand.

Did I really want to shake a hand that had touched a goat and who knew what else? No way. But I didn't particularly want to offend him, either. We shook.

"My friend Paul was hurt."

His brow wrinkled. "Paul?"

I nodded. "Ethelwulf sent him to help me, and he got hurt by Gerrard." I held up the box. Inside, Paul lay on his side, sleeping. He snored like a bull frog.

The ogre sniffed. "I think I know Paul."

"Will someone help him? I know he did something wrong, but he's hurt. He's a good person— er, cricket— or turner or wizard or whatever he is."

He stared at the box. He frowned, his expression turned grim. I thought for sure he would tell me there was no chance in hell. Finally he said, "I'll find someone."

The goat bleated softly as it chewed on the rope and Thorn pulled it out of its mouth.

"So what's with the goat?" I asked.

"Maxi?" Thorn said, rubbing the goat's side. I nodded. "He was to take the place of the boy."

"Savion?" I asked, surprised. What did he mean the goat was to take the place of Savion? Unless . . .

"I was right. You guys knew Savion was the focus," I said, wondering if I should work up the energy to be mad or not.

Thorn sighed, and the room smelled briefly like the inside of a garbage can. "We thought it," he said, "but we did not know it."

"I messed up," I said. I fiddle with the latch on Paul's box.

The ogre said nothing. He patted the goat, brushed the fur on the goat's side.

"I should have stopped him. I could have stopped him. I have the powers of Council. But it didn't work. What good is magic if it doesn't work?"

"Maybe it did work," Thorn said.

"It didn't. All I did was push him off me."

"Maybe that's all you wanted to do."

I shook my head. This was all too surreal. I was sitting in a room I'd seen inside a pot, in a city that didn't exist, talking to an impossible creature about my failure in using a weapon I didn't want anyway.

Maybe that's all you wanted to do. What did he know about what I wanted? What did anyone know about what I wanted? I didn't want this job. It was forced on me. I didn't want magic. I was born with it. Nobody ever asked me what I wanted.

I wanted a normal life. No spell-turners. No elves. No ogres. No magic. A normal life with normal friends. I wanted a best friend. I wanted a boyfriend. I didn't want to worry about what I could and couldn't say to them. I didn't want magic to ruin my friendships.

What did they know about what I wanted?

The ogre was silent. Though his eyelids were heavy, I was beginning to realize he wasn't as dumb as he looked.

"It's not about want," Thorn said. "Maybe you already have all that you need."

Great. Now the ogre was getting philosophical. Could this get any weirder?

Unfortunately his words reminded me of Rory and that Rolling Stones song. And the sweet sound of his voice singing to me.

Guilt swept over me. I'd told him I would call him later. I'd planned to see him at school in the morning. I didn't think it likely I was going to school again any time soon. I couldn't live at home and go to school while Gerrard was out there. From Rory's perspective it would look like I was avoiding him. I wondered if there was a way I could get a message to him, telling him not to worry, telling him I'd had to go on a last minute trip. But with Savion missing from school as well, I wasn't sure if that was a good idea. Gerrard would have to notify the school of Savion's absence; if Rory heard Savion was away at the same time I'd wordlessly disappeared? Yeah, I was pretty sure he'd be jealous and that would be the end of any hope I had for being his girlfriend.

The bedroom door opened abruptly and Rhiannon strode out. "Coming?" she asked as she strode to the front door. There was something urgent in her eyes that had me up and moving quickly to the door.

"Take care," I said to Thorn. "It was . . . nice talking to you." I waved.

"Good night," he said. "Maximillion says good night, too."

I hurried to keep up with Rhiannon as she stalked down the hallway and hurried down the stairs.

"Is something wrong?" I asked, following her down the street. "Is Ethelwulf okay?"

She stopped in the middle of the cobblestoned street. People brushed past us, but didn't look twice. She spoke in a low voice, "The Elders are restoring Ethelwulf's powers. He'll be on his feet again in a few days."

That was a huge relief. "So what's wrong?"

"The Elders have cancelled the mission. We've been pulled off the case. They're not allowing anyone to go after Lebrun."

CHAPTER SIXTEEN

"WHAT?" I BLINKED. I hoped she was kidding. I waited for her to laugh. "This is a joke, right?"

She started to walk away. "Come on. We can talk about it at my place."

"Did you tell them about the focus? About what he's doing to Savion?" I asked, chasing after her once again.

She didn't answer, which I took to mean she'd tell me once we got to her place. Hopefully.

We went inside by way of a panelled, shiny lacquered bright red door that was sandwiched between a bakery and a jewellery store. Both stores carried special items I'd never seen in the human world. We went up to two flights of stairs to her top floor apartment, number 303.

Her place wasn't at all what I would have expected for a turner— not that I knew what to expect, given my limited experience with all things magical— and yet it was totally appropriate. Exactly right for Rhiannon.

The walls were white with wooden floors that had been whitewashed. All the furniture was made of metal with fat foam cushions in white. All shelves were metal. Where kitchen cabinets should have been, there were stainless steel shelves instead. Brightly coloured metal sculptures were dotted throughout. The one-bedroom apartment had a light and airy feeling to it. White furry rugs thrown on the floor and chesterfield kept the place from feeling cold.

All of that was nice, but what captured my attention was the ceiling, a field of twinkling stars behind a rising moon.

"Come in," she said, shrugging off her long grey military-style coat. She hung it on a coat tree. My own jacket was somewhere at Savion's house.

She glanced back to see me still staring at the ceiling.

"Pretty cool, huh? This place used to belong to an air turner. She let me keep the ceiling when she left. It changes with the sky of the human world, much like the sky above the Sanctuary."

"So the Sanctuary is underground?"

"No. It's just somewhere else."

"Where?"

"I don't think it's really anywhere in particular. It's just everywhere the rest of the world is not." She opened the door to a closet with deep shelves piled with boxes and linens. She pulled out a sheet and a thick quilt. "Do you understand?"

"I'm not sure I do."

"I'm sorry I can't explain it better."

I shrugged. "I never was very good at understanding philosophical ideas."

"How about math?"

"Math I can handle."

"All right. Then think of the Sanctuary as zero. It's mathematically possible, but in reality, zero is the absence of something. You have a dollar and I take it away; you are left with the absence of a dollar."

"You're saying the Sanctuary is the absence of something?"

She nodded.

"What's it the absence of?"

"Why, it is the absence of everything and everywhere else."

"Okay," I said. "I understand that from a mathematical point of view, but not from a geographical point of view."

She smiled. "That's because it's not about geography."

"Huh?"

"Geography is the science of physical space. The Sanctuary isn't about science or physical space."

"Then what's it about?"

She grinned. "Magic."

I was getting the feeling I wouldn't ever fully understand how or where the Sanctuary existed, but the beginnings of a theory were forming.

"So let me get this straight — the Sanctuary exists magically everywhere that reality is not."

She nodded. "That's right."

"And the doors to the Sanctuary?"

"Are places that are magically tied to reality."

"Interesting." There was no way I would ever fully understand this stuff, and I wasn't sure I wanted to. I mean, the very idea that I was currently standing somewhere that was mathematically possible, but not physically possible, was starting to blow my mind.

While she made a bed for me out of the chaise, I gently put Paul's box on the kitchen counter peninsula. It was comforting to hear him snore, but I missed his company. He needed a healer. Someone who could repair his tiny leg. I hoped Thorn found someone by morning. Merlin only knew what Paul would be like when he woke up.

I watched Rhiannon toss aside pillows, and flap the sheets in stiff, short bursts. I couldn't believe the Elders had cancelled the mission when we were so close. We should be storming over there, taking Gerrard by surprise. How could we back down now?

"Did you tell them about Savion?" I asked.

She snorted. "They said he doesn't matter."

"But— But what will happen to him if his father keeps pulling spells through him?"

"If he was human, eventually the spells would deplete him of enough energy that he would get sick and never recover."

"But he's a turner."

She nodded slowly. "He'll become a full turner in a matter of weeks. If his father continues to pull spells through him . . . " She stopped, and took a breath. "Understand this is purely conjecture because no one has done this before. The school of thought is Lebrun's powers will double once he combines his powers with his son."

And that would be bad. Gerrard was already more powerful than most.

"Wrong." The voice came from across the room. I almost didn't hear it. "Mel, help me up."

Paul could be loud when he wanted to be. He made no exception when I lifted him out of his box and carried him to Rhiannon's coffee table, and he complained the whole time. She put a pillow on the table and I gently laid Paul on it.

"What do you know about this, Paul—" she said. She started to say his full name, but caught herself.

"Enough," he spit back. "More than enough."

"Then start talking." She lowered herself to a chair. I sat on the chaise, which was ready to be my bed.

"Why should I? You're not going to believe me anyway."

She clenched her jaw, shifted her position on the chair. "It's not by coincidence that you were chosen to keep an eye on Mel, is it? Of all the creatures in the world, Ethelwulf chose you, a neutralized wizard, an outlaw— a murderer."

He cringed. "See, I knew you wouldn't believe me."

"But that's just it. You should have been neutralized, and yet Ethelwulf made you into a cricket—"

"Before being a cricket, he was a mouse," I interjected.

She arched an eyebrow at me, and then turned back to Paul. "You've been working for Ethelwulf for quite some time, then, haven't you? Now why would he do that? Why would he think you didn't deserve to be excommunicated from the magical community, but made into a spy instead?"

"Maybe because you dumb turners got it all wrong. That's why. He was the only one who believed me."

"But— If— " She shook her head. "If we got it all wrong, then who killed Vincent?"

He laid there, staring up at her, his antennae twitching. She stared back, blinking, daring him to speak. Memories were being recalled, but not shared.

"Who's Vincent?" I asked.

No one answered me.

"So you're saying you didn't pull the spell—" she started.

"I did," he finished.

"Then—"

"It was an accident."

"Who's Vincent?" I asked again. Would I ever find out what was going on?

She shook her head. "But that's not possible. We found no evidence of a focus being used. You must have destroyed it. No other magic was found, except the spells that went through your brother."

"Wait," I said, standing up with a bad feeling. "What's going on? What's this about?"

"A blood turner doesn't require a focus," Paul said.

"Yes, they do," Rhiannon said. "All turners require a focus. Power requires a channel."

"Blood turner?" I said. "Is that what a wizard is?"

Rhiannon snorted. "You told her you're a wizard?"

"That's not what a wizard is," Paul said to me. "And not everyone needs a focus."

"Actually," I said, "he might be right about that. I've never been able to use a focus, but I've still channelled power from my fingertips. Now will someone please tell me what happened?"

For a moment no one said anything. Then Rhiannon said, "It's your story, Paul."

"I know," he said. "I just don't know where to start."

He sounded upset, and if he was upset, then it was probably because I'd been insisting on knowing the whole story. I'd pushed the situation and I shouldn't have. But by the sounds of it, Paul was the only source of information we had about turners pulling spells through others. He was our only hope for helping Savion. I had no choice but to push him.

"Let's start at the beginning," I said. "Who's Vincent?"

"Vincent was my twin brother," Paul said. "He was the wild one. I was the cool, level-headed one."

Memories of Paul's dramatic moments flitted through my mind. I found his statement hard to believe. But we could argue the definition of "level-headed" later.

Paul continued, "Vincent got himself tangled up with the wrong crowd. He was going to leave us to go join them. I got wind of it and went to stop him."

"Black magic users," I guessed.

"Worse."

"There's worse than black magic?"

No one answered me. I supposed they didn't have to. The answer was written all over Rhiannon's grim face.

"Anyway, we had a fight. One of his new 'buddies' came along to find out what was taking him so long, and that's when it went bad. I ended up fighting for my life. Vincent almost got away. I tried to use a binding spell on him, but he was bleeding from our fight. The spell went right through him. He was dead before he hit the ground."

Oh. Wow. How horrible.

"It wouldn't have hurt him at all if he'd been a blood turner like me."

"But why didn't Ethelwulf stand up for you?" I asked. "If it was just an accident, then why were you punished?"

"He did. The Elders didn't care. They only wanted me stopped so I wouldn't do it again and they wanted to set an example so others wouldn't get any ideas."

"Black magic is black magic," Rhiannon said.

"But you're on the Council," I said. "Don't you care about the truth?"

"Actually, our job is not to judge. We are only to follow evidence, find the wrong-doers, and bring them before the Elders," she said.

"You should care about what you're doing."

"We do. It's why we take the job seriously. It's why not many turners are willing to work for Council. After this incident with Paulinus, Ethelwulf pushed hard for evidence to brought before the Elders. It's why we needed Lebrun's focus before we can get a neutralization."

"But Savion is his focus," I said.

"You must be mistaken," she said.

"Don't mind her, Mel. It's virtually unheard of to use a living being as focus," Paul said. "In my case, it was an accident. In Lebrun's case, it is deliberate."

"We have to help him."

"The Elders have decided to let Lebrun go free," she said. "They don't want him stopped."

"But Savion might die. And what about my Gran? We can't just leave her with him."

"If I'm understanding Paulinus correctly, whether Savion lives or dies will depend on what type of turner he is. But understand this: if Savion dies, Lebrun will no longer have a focus for his black magic. And that may be the Elders' plan."

"On the other hand," Paul said, "if the boy is a blood turner, Lebrun will be a thousand times more powerful. That's quite a gamble the Elders are willing to take."

"Maybe the increased power is not a risk at all," Rhiannon said. "Maybe they know something." She turned to me. "Turners tend to surround themselves with their element, it's the most important thing to them, even to almost-turners. You've been to Savion's room. Can you think of what his element might be?"

I shook my head. "That's ridiculous. If I'm a blood turner— and I think there's a good chance I am— then you're saying my room would be decorated in blood. That's disgusting!"

"But I'll bet you are surrounded by blood." She held up a finger to stop me from arguing. "I'll bet you have quite a few pictures of your family in your room. I'll bet you spend a lot of time thinking about your family. I'll bet you're never far from your family at all."

She was right about my room. There were pictures of my parents all over the place. I put them up so I would remember what they looked like. But what if she was right? What if it was because I was a blood turner?

The locket containing the pictures of my parents felt warm against my breastbone.

"Nothing is more important to a blood turner than family," Paul said quietly.

His family. My family. Maybe they were right. Gerrard was a blood turner, and his house was practically a shrine to his late wife.

"Can you think of what Savion's element might be?" Rhiannon asked.

I thought back to his room, his very blue room with the games, television, chesterfield, mini-fridge, the quilt with sailboats, the bathroom, the fish tank—

"Water," I answered. "I think it's water." And I told them about his room.

"Could his element be blood?" she asked.

I shook my head. "He resents his father. Or maybe he resents how much time his father spends working. Whatever. It's almost like he's afraid of his father. He misses his mom, though."

"From what I saw, he was loyal to his father."

My stomach twisted as the feeling of betrayal arose within me. I couldn't believe Savion chose to follow his father.

Mmm." She leaned back in the chair.

"We must be sure," Paul said.

"We can't let him die," I said. "We have to save him."

"The Elders have taken us off the case," Rhiannon said. She sounded tired.

"Then I'll go alone." I didn't know how, I didn't know where, but I knew I had to try. I wouldn't leave Gran to die.

"You mustn't," Rhiannon rose out of the chair. "Don't you see? You're a blood turner, he's a blood turner. Together, he could be ten times more powerful."

"A thousand," Paul corrected.

She looked at him. "I thought you were exaggerating."

"Sorry."

"You're not?"

"It's Ethelwulf's estimate. We're charting unknown waters here. But think about it. If a simple spell can go so wrong when elements clash, then it only makes sense the power would be magnified when elements are the same."

"But a thousand times?"

"It's like exponents," I interrupted. "Ten to the power of one is ten. Ten to the power of two is a hundred. Ten to the power of three is a thousand."

"Yeah, sure. Let's go with that," Paul said. "Math show-off."

"It works as long as the base is the same," Rhiannon said.

"The base is the same," I said. "Blood turner power. My power, his power, and the combined power all stacked together. A thousand times the power."

"Holy crap," Paul said. "Ethelwulf was right."

"Which is why you're not going anywhere," Rhiannon said sternly. Her pale skin was as white as the walls.

"Which is why I have to go. I'm the perfect focus for Gerrard. How can he resist me?"

She stared at me like I was nuts. I guess maybe I was. I didn't stop to think about it. I was too scared to.

"It's perfect," I continued. "We go in, lure Gerrard's powers out of Savion, and before Gerrard sinks his claws into me, hit him with everything we've got."

"That's so nutty it just might work," Paul said, sounding surprised. "I love the pink hair, by the way."

Rhiannon scowled, startled by his comment. "It might," she said, ignoring his compliment, except to glare at him. "But if we're not quick enough or strong enough, he'll kill us all once he has you."

"Yeah. There's that," Paul said. His disappointment stemmed from more than just her pointing out the flaw in his plan.

"Which is why we're not doing it," she said.

"But I am," I said. "I don't care if he takes me, if it means Gran is saved, if we can stop him."

"Are you crazy?" she asked.

"It's our best shot," I pointed out. I let my eyes plead with Rhiannon, begging for her to see the sense in it.

"I don't like it," she said. She turned on her heel, stalked to her bedroom and slammed the door shut behind her.

"I guess we're back to square one," I said with a sigh. I shut off the light and climbed under the quilt. The piles of furs on the foamy chaise warmed up quickly, and I was steadily heading for dreamland.

"Actually," Paul said in the dark, "she never said no."

Realizing he was right, I fell asleep with a smile.

CHAPTER SEVENTEEN

IN THE MORNING, after I woke, for a long time I just stayed on the chaise and watched the ceiling. There wasn't much to see beyond the beauty of the endless blue sky, but occasionally birds would fly by. One time it was a single bird, another time it was a pair, and once a small flock of white doves went by. It was beautiful, peaceful, and I lay there, warm under the covers, unwilling to move.

I heard Rhiannon wake and rumble through her morning routine, so I thought I'd best get up as well. She came out of her room and handed me a coat of navy blue wool.

"Come on," she said with a smile. "Let's go."

"Go where?" I asked, but she'd already left.

I quickly yanked on my shoes and hurried after her. I had a feeling I knew where we were going, but I didn't want to lose sight of Rhiannon just in case I was wrong. Excitement filled me as our path along the cobblestones took us toward my mother's store.

Even at this early hour, the streets were busy with turners and other creatures going about their daily business. I saw an ogre carrying a burlap sack over his shoulder and for a moment I thought it was Thorn. I lifted my hand to wave, but the ogre's nose was crooked where Thorn's was straight. Turners in long dark coats and pointed toed shoes darted in and out of the shops with brown paper packages bundled in their arms. The air smelled of fresh cinnamon rolls and greasy sausage, but there was a tinge of frost to the air. I was glad for Rhiannon's coat. Even as early as it was, the Sanctuary, this place, felt right. I felt like I could belong here.

The lights were off inside A Matter of Focus, the objects in the window display concealed in shadow. Rhiannon slipped a skeleton key out of her coat pocket and unlocked the door. A bell chimed over our heads as the door opened and we went inside.

"Wait here," Rhiannon said. She slipped into the darkness. When the lights came on, I could see why she'd told me to wait.

My mother's shop was like an antique store with tables all around piled with trinkets. One wrong move and I could have knocked over a tray of china cups and saucers.

"This is my mother's focus shop?" I asked.

"You sound surprised."

"Well, yeah. I thought my mother sold focuses. This looks like an antique store." I caught sight of a glass case of junk jewellery and wrinkled my nose.

"One never knows what object is going to be the right focus for a turner until one finds it."

"Seriously? A tea cup could be a focus?" I plucked a rose patterned china cup off a table and examined it.

Rhiannon shrugged. "Certainly a white turner like your Gran might prefer to work with a tea cup."

"I can't imagine waving this around to do magic," I said and waved the tea cup as if waving a small flag. "Let alone to stir potions."

"You wouldn't use to stir a potion. You would use to serve a potion. Or perhaps for divination."

"What— like reading tea leaves and stuff?"

"Precisely."

I put the cup back with a sigh and roamed around the tables.

"So, this is where my mother would sell focuses to turners?" I tried to picture my mother here, but couldn't.

"It was also a repair shop."

"A repair shop? What did she repair?"

"Focuses."

"She repaired focuses? I don't understand. Do focuses need to be repaired?"

"Periodically. If a high number of spells pass through a focus in a short amount of time, the focus loses focus. The spells become less clear, as they pick up residue from the spells cast previously."

I stopped my wandering in front of a case of carved wooden sticks. Wands.

"That's why you wanted Gerrard's focus. To read the residue of the spells pulled through it," I said quietly.

Rhiannon's mouth was a grim line. She didn't answer. She didn't need to. Ethelwulf had already told me that's what they were going to do.

"What will happen to Savion once you remove the spells from him? Will he still have his own power? Will he still be a turner?"

She looked like she was going to say something then changed her mind. "I don't know. Removing the spells will be tricky enough, but untangling them from Savion's own power . . . I think it safe to say he will be forever changed by all this. We all will be."

Her words gave me an odd feeling. I knew she was right, that others would be changed by this mission to capture Gerrard— I had only to think of Thorn to know that— but it felt weird to me. I'd thought I was the only one to suffer because of the sorcerer.

"Why is he doing this? Gerrard, I mean. Why did he kill my mother and the other turners?"

She shook her head. "Perhaps only he will ever know why he does what he does."

"He won't expose us to humans, will he?"

Rhiannon gasped. "Why would you say that?"

I wanted to tell her she didn't look into Gerrard's eyes, I did. But instead, I shrugged. "He seems to be punishing us. He's certainly reducing our numbers."

Rhiannon was quiet while I examined a rack of broomsticks. I'd thought I would find some trace of my mother in this store, some piece of her— the piece of her she'd kept hidden from me all this time— but there was nothing. Nothing about this place said "Lavinia Caldwell was here." I'd thought I might see a piece of myself. Oh, I knew my mother would never have tacked a picture of me to the wall, not when she was working undercover and wanted to keep this life a secret from me. But I thought something in this place might resonate with me, that there might be something here a turner mother would give to her daughter.

If anything, this trip to the store only made my mother even more of a stranger.

I headed for the door.

"All finished?" Rhiannon asked, following me. She fished the key out of her pocket.

"Who will look after this place now?" I asked, waiting while she locked up.

A look passed over her face— of regret or something like it— and then was gone.

"No one's been chosen," she said. She turned the key and the lock slid into place.

***

* * *

On the way back to the apartment, Rhiannon stopped at the bakery and picked up breakfast: coffee, juice, and sandwiches made from cinnamon rolls and sausage rounds. We were sitting at her kitchen counter eating the confections when there was a knock at the door.

Rhiannon seemed confused, but put her fork down and went to see who was there.

I picked up the glass of juice and sniffed, breathing in the sweet and tart tones of cranberry and maple.

"Ethelwulf!" she cried, and I nearly dropped the glass.

Indeed, the elf was here and currently caught in the turner's embrace. She released him and ushered him straight to the chesterfield. He leaned heavily on his cane, crouched more than usual, hobbling slower than usual. He appeared pale and tired, even more so in the striped blue and white pyjamas and furry slippers he wore.

Seeing him up and walking, I felt elated, but seeing him so depleted of energy, of vitality, of life, I felt horrible. Just how close had we been to losing him?

"Can I get you a bite to eat?" she asked as she propped him up with pillows and covered his lap with the quilt.

"No, no," he insisted with a cough. His voice sounded hoarse. "A cup of tea will be sufficient." As he spoke, he closely examined Paul's injury.

Rhiannon nodded and went straight to work in the kitchen.

The elf hovered his hand over Paul. A warm glow spread through his hands, the rings on his fingers becoming dark shadows against the light.

"Leave me," Paul murmured without opening his eyes. "Leave me to die."

Ethelwulf chuckled. "There's not much chance of that, old friend."

"Face it. My time has come. My number is up. My life is over." His head rolled back, his limbs went limp.

Ethelwulf leaned in close to the cricket, the glow reflecting orange light against his pale skin, and whispered, "But your work here is not done."

Paul opened one eye. "It's not?"

Rhiannon clucked her tongue from across the room. "Ethelwulf, you shouldn't be wasting what little energy you have."

He ignored her and continued to speak to Paul. "Lebrun is still out there."

"You don't need me for that." Paul flopped back, eyes closed again.

"Perhaps not. But certainly Melantha needs you."

His eyes flew open. "No, she doesn't. Soon she'll be a full turner. And then what? You'll send me to spy on someone else? I can't take it anymore, Ethelwulf. You don't know what it's like to put your life on the line day in and day out. Have you ever stared up into the eyes of a hungry cat? Dodged high heels, steel toes or rubber soles? It's not pleasant. I'd rather die right here, right now, than be a lizard's walking appetizer or a smudge on the bottom of a shoe." He pointed one foreleg at the elf, then flopped back, his antennae sprawled out dramatically.

"Hmm. Yes, I can imagine it must be a dangerous life," Ethelwulf said.

"That's right."

"Always watching your back—"

"Uh-huh."

"Working hard to survive and help others—"

"You betcha."

"As any Council member would do."

"Yep— hey! I don't work for Council. I work for you."

Ethelwulf waived a hand. "Semantics. The bottom line is this: you enjoy this work or you would never have agreed to work with me in the first place. You love the thrill; you love helping people. And nothing is going to stop you. Not for long."

"But my leg—"

"Haven't you noticed?"

"What?"

The elf grinned. The cricket slowly curled his black body, turning to have a gander at his fixed leg. I couldn't help but smile as Paul gaped at the elf's sly handiwork.

"What!" He rolled over and crawled in circles, watching his leg in action. "Ha! Ha! It's fixed! You old fox. Wait— This is going to cost me, isn't it." He crawled backwards on the pillow so he could better see Ethelwulf.

"Normally, the pain you endured would stand as payment already served, and indeed it has, but I must also ask a favour of you old friend." The old man's cheer faded into serious tones as he spoke.

Also sober, the cricket sighed. "After what you just did for me, how can I say no?"

"I admit my timing with this couldn't be worse, but as I depleted the very last of my energy repairing your limb, I have no alternate choice." He accepted the tea cup and saucer from Rhiannon. She sat in the chair opposite him.

Paul heaved another dramatic sigh. "Okay. What is it?"

"Wait—" I interjected. "What do you mean you've depleted the last of your energy? What does that mean?"

Ethelwulf's gaze flickered to me, and then to Rhiannon as he sipped from his steaming cup of tea. They both frowned.

"Gerrard Lebrun's attack was designed to suck up all the magical energy it could get," he said. His face was solemn and full of regret as he remembered.

"An energy bomb," Rhiannon summarized. "If Ethelwulf hadn't blocked it, if it had hit the rest of us, we'd all be depleted as well."

The elf nodded. "It must have taken him months to build that spell. But you forget. I wasn't the only one hit by it."

"How is he?" she asked.

"Fair, under the circumstances. But I'm afraid he will lose his leg."

Rhiannon's face fell. I asked, "Who?" but I already had a bad feeling.

"Thorn," Ethelwulf answered. I remembered the ogre's bandaged leg.

"But— what's wrong with him? Why does he have to lose his leg? Won't he heal?"

Ethelwulf took a breath as he composed his response. "There's a little magic inside every human. There's a little more in turners, elves and others, along with the awareness of that magic. But ogres, trolls and a few other creatures are mostly magic. Thorn tried to push me out of the way, but when the energy bomb hit him, it was no different than a human stepping on a land mine."

"Really?" My voice was small and far away as I chased away the mental picture of an ogre leg exploded open.

"I'm afraid so. The Elders are with him now, but I'm afraid there just isn't that much to work with." He sipped tea. "And I'm afraid that's why we've been taken off the case. It'll be weeks before my energy is restored, and Thorn's recovery will take months. We can't go without seven of us, and it's too late to bring in anyone new."

"It's not too late," I blurted. "Bring in two more people. If we work quickly, there's still a chance we can catch them at the cottage."

A silent conversation passed between them in one glance.

"It's not that simple," Rhiannon said.

"What does that mean?"

"It means," Paul said, "there are enemies everywhere. Anyone could be a black magic turner, and we can't risk bringing in a sympathizer."

"So don't," I said.

"But it will take months—"

"Years," Ethelwulf corrected.

"Years to do background checks," Paul finished.

"But—" I tried.

"Even if we found someone, their magic has to be compatible with ours," Rhiannon said.

"Ethelwulf has spent years building this group of seven," Paul said. "Not to mention how long it took to get the goat."

There had to be a way. There just had to. I wasn't going to be content with letting Lebrun get away with my mother's murder. But most of all, I couldn't get the last image I had of Gran out of my head.

"Why seven?" I asked. "It's a prime number. Is that it?"

"That's part of it." Ethelwulf nodded. "It's enough to produce the combined power needed to overcome black magic, but not so much that we lose control."

Five was all that was available from the seven, which was also a prime number, but apparently not enough to overcome black magic. The next prime number was eleven. I tried to visualize eleven beings wielding magic as they fought against one black magic sorcerer. It would be a lot of bodies to jam into one room. And a lot of power. He was right. I could see them quickly losing control.

"But you still have five, right?" I said. "Maybe it will be enough." I had to get them to at least try.

"It won't be enough," Rhiannon said.

But I noticed the hope Ethelwulf was trying to hide. And I had to go for it.

"Take me and Paul," I blurted before I lost my nerve.

"What?" Paul and Rhiannon cried simultaneously.

I looked at them. "Five plus two equals seven."

"But you don't have any powers," Rhiannon said. "Either one of you."

"Yet," I corrected.

"Paul's been neutralized," she said.

I felt my face flush hot with frustration. "But Vincent's death was an accident."

Paul's antennae sagged. "I ended a life by using magic, Melantha. The Council views it the same as murder."

"Not all of the Council," Ethelwulf corrected.

"No," Paul agreed. "Not all."

"Because it was an accident, I was able to convince the Elders to give you a second chance."

"You were?" Paul's antennae picked up.

"Why else would I send you out on solo missions?" He smiled. "The Elders listened when I explained how the accident happened. They agreed that if you could show yourself to be selfless and willing to help others without assistance, then you would have both your body and powers restored."

"You were selfless?" Rhiannon asked. "When? How?"

Paul looked at Ethelwulf. "Yeah. When? How?"

The elf grinned. "When you put yourself in harm's way to help Melantha."

Paul's antennae drooped. "Well, I didn't think I was doing something selfless. I was only trying to help."

"I think that's the point," I said dryly.

"Yeah, I narrowly avoided getting squashed by the sorcerer's Italian leather." Paul snorted.

"And so, you shall be rewarded," Ethelwulf said.

"You mean it?"

The elf nodded.

"Jiminy Crickets! No flippin' way!"

The elf responded with a nod and smile that went all the way up to the twinkle in his eyes despite his exhausted condition.

"Woohoo!" Paul cried as he did a back flip. "When can we get started?"

He crawled to the edge closest to Ethelwulf and looked up at him like a puppy expecting a big juicy bone. I think his butt was wagging.

It was the happiest news I'd heard in days. Maybe months.

There was only one person who was less than thrilled.

"Congratulations," Rhiannon said sourly as she rose off the chair. "Aren't you lucky? You're getting away with murder."

She stormed to her bedroom and slammed the door, leaving us in a stunned silence.

CHAPTER EIGHTEEN

THE ELF CLEARED his throat, the first to break the silence, but it was the cricket who spoke first.

"I guess she still hates me," Paul said, his voice void of happiness.

"She doesn't hate you," I muttered, casting a glance at the closed bedroom door.

"Oh, yes, she does."

"My friend," Ethelwulf said. "Melantha is correct. You wouldn't be in this room if Rhiannon hated you."

"Maybe," Paul said, turning around on the pillow so he could stare at the bedroom door. "Or maybe she hates me."

"She's angry and she blames you, but she doesn't hate you," I explained. "There's a difference."

"Oh really? So you're what? Her psychologist now?"

"No."

"So how would you know?"

"Because she sounds exactly the way I sound every time I fight with Gran."

I could hear every fight with Gran so clearly. I was so angry— still was angry— but I no longer blamed Gran. It took seeing Paul's point of view to make me understand how Gran must have felt.

"But I don't hate her," I said softly.

"She will be happy to hear that," Ethelwulf said.

"She's all right?" I asked, filled with hope. I'd been much to afraid of his answer to ask before. But if he thought we had a shot at saving her, then perhaps there was a chance she was all right.

"She's staying at a farmhouse surrounded by butterfly-filled gardens.

She's not unhappy there, but she's looking forward to returning home."

"Why do I sense there's more to it than that?"

"Because you have good instincts and you're finally listening to them." He smiled.

"The orb. I know he has it."

Ethelwulf nodded sadly. "To bring Alberta home, we must get the orb back."

I suddenly caught on to his plan. "Is that our new mission?"

Ethelwulf nodded. "Indeed."

"Wait—" Paul said, turning to look up at the elf. "You seriously did not just agree to let her fight Lebrun, did you? Are you nuts?"

"No, no. A little short on power, but the noggin's still good." He knocked his knuckles on his temple, smiling all the while. "I think."

"But she's just a child!"

"Hey," I interjected. "I thought you agreed with going after Lebrun."

"Actually," Paul said, "I said it might work, not that I ever agreed you should go."

I frowned. The cricket had turned on me, and it stung.

"Look, I'm sorry," Paul said. He softened his tone. "Your heart's in the right place, even if your brain isn't. You'll make a great addition to the team someday, but you said yourself you don't know any magic."

"I know some," I argued, unhappy with Paul's idea of where my brain was. I tried to tell myself he was just worried about me, but that didn't make it sting any less.

I wondered if Paul's switching sides had anything to do with Rhiannon's reaction to him getting his body back. Was he doing this to please her?

Gran hadn't been able to teach me much, in part because I wouldn't let her after my mother died, and in part because much of what she'd tried to teach didn't work for me. She had white turner powers. I was pretty much convinced I had anything but.

I wasn't so certain I had blood turner powers, either. From what I'd learned in my lessons, blood turners were rare. Like one in thousand turners. It seemed like too much of a coincidence that in the same few days I find out I might be a blood turner, I meet two other blood turners — Paul and Gerrard.

"If I may," Ethelwulf said, "you will not be going after Lebrun, as that has been forbidden, you will be merely rescuing Alberta. But you didn't hear that from me."

"You mean it?" I asked hopefully.

"You old fox," Paul said with approval.

"We'd better get going," Ethelwulf said. "You're going to be quite busy."

He set the pillow on the coffee table, and with a grunt, and obvious effort, he pushed off the chesterfield to stand leaning on his cane.

"Where are we going?" I asked, glancing at the bedroom door.

"Paul has an appointment with the Elders."

"I'm getting my body back? Now?"

The elf blinked. "When else?"

"Woohoo!" He back flipped on the pillow again. "Wait— Back up the truck. Why am I going to be busy? You don't mean to carry out this suicidal mission?"

"Not me. But you will."

"No way. I can't!"

"And why not?"

"Come on. I'm not exactly a model citizen."

"Paul, we all make mistakes," the elf said. "The wise learn from their mistakes so as not to repeat them. Are you wise, Paul?"

Paul grunted. "By that definition, I guess."

"Do you want Melantha to be wise as well?"

"Why wouldn't I?"

"Then do not be afraid of mistakes— neither yours or someone else's. Fear only those who choose not to see the errors of their ways."

Paul grunted again. "I'm hearing you, but it's a lot to ask."

Ethelwulf smiled. "Is it? It's no more than a leap of faith. And by the looks of you, I'd say you're pretty good at making leaps."

Ethelwulf made his slow trek to the door. Paul hopped down and bounded after him.

"What about Rhiannon?" I asked. She'd taken me in, given me a place to stay, and looked after me. She even made me breakfast. It just didn't feel right leaving her behind like this. We hadn't even tried to talk to her.

Ethelwulf stopped and half-turned towards me.

"Rhiannon," he began, but paused for a deep breath. "She knows she's always welcome to join us when she's ready."

I had a feeling his words weren't just meant for me.

I didn't like it. It felt wrong to leave her somehow, and I wasn't entirely happy with Paul flipping sides on me like that, but how could I not be there for Paul's big moment? I followed Ethelwulf out of the apartment, scooping up Paul so he could ride on my sleeve.

The main street was alive with morning activity. My heart stirred, still amazed there were so many turners, elves and other magical beings in the world. We turned off the bright, cobblestone street to an alley where the bright sky was blocked by the tall buildings. The alley seemed to go on forever, and by the time we emerged at the other end, the sky had covered over with clouds.

The alley opened up to a wide, grassy field. We were headed for the forest of evergreens on the other side. The grass was up to my knees and made scratching sounds against my jeans as we marched towards the dark woods. Crickets chirped in the distance and from his perch on my arm, Paul answered them.

A cool breeze blew past, passing right through my sweater. The wind smelled clean, but promised rain. I was grateful when we reached the shelter of the trees, although my gratitude was temporary.

From the moment we stepped off the main street, I became aware of a sneaky feeling rising up out of the shadows. It was a creepy sensation. I felt like I was being watched or being followed. It was the kind of feeling that sneaks up on you on a Halloween night or at twilight when the veil between light and darkness grows thin.

"Where are we going?" My voice fell flat, deadened by the dense trees and the thick layer of decayed brush under our feet. Crows cawed high in the treetops, laughing as though they could sense my growing fear.

"You'll see," Paul answered, though he didn't sound happy to be going there.

I looked back over my shoulder. The busy street and bright sky seemed so far away, though we hadn't been hiking for very long. "H-How much farther do we have to go?"

"We're almost there."

I clung to his words, my only comfort, as mist swirled around my ankles, and the eerie feeling intensified.

"This is some kind of magical alarm system, isn't it?" I asked. The trees thinned, almost as if they parted so we could pass through, opening to reveal a large, misty glen, which had at the centre a cemetery. A tall, wrought-iron fence surrounded the cemetery.

"Of sorts," Ethelwulf said.

He stared up at the imposing, elaborate gates.

"Melantha, perhaps it would be best if you waited out here," he said, not removing his eyes from the black gates.

"What? Why?" I so did not want to be left alone out here for them.

"The things you will experience inside these gates can be frightening to children."

"They're frightening for adults," Paul said with a shudder.

I knew they were probably right. I sensed it as much as I sensed the darkness rising with the mist. I saw it as plainly as I saw the arches of the gates with their twin frowns, the iron bars their rotting teeth. And yet, given the choice of being swallowed up by the cemetery's jaws or waiting out here in the soughing trees, I wanted to stay with them.

"I'm not a child."

"It won't be good."

I shook my head. "I'm coming with you."

Ethelwulf sighed. "I can't promise you'll either like or understand what you'll experience in here. The ceremony Paul has to endure is—" He pursed his lips. "I should have left you in Rhiannon's care. You can head back there now. Yes, yes. Maybe that would be best."

He took me by the elbow and tried to escort me to the glen. Paul used the opportunity to jump to the elf's arm.

"I'm staying," I said, yanking my elbow out of his grip. "Paul is my friend. I'm here to support him."

Ethelwulf frowned, his displeasure evident. "Once you pass through these gates you won't be able to change your mind."

I nodded my understanding. I glanced at the cemetery. It was easily a couple of football fields of mist-covered tombstones. I looked away.

The cool wind soughed through the trees, sending goose bumps over my arms. The bushes rattled behind me, and as I turned, a hand reached out and grabbed my arm.

A terrified scream escaped my mouth. I lunged for the elf.

"Hush," he said. "It's okay."

I looked over my shoulder to see Rhiannon emerging from the bushes.

"I didn't mean to frighten you," she said. "I tripped on a tree root. I never did like coming here."

I nodded, my pulse caught in my throat. "This place gives me the creeps."

"To say the least," she said. She'd changed into teal jeans and a white cable-knit sweater with a blue and green tartan scarf looped around her neck. The outfit worked well with her new blond hair colour.

"And for a good reason," Ethelwulf interjected. "This is not like cemeteries you may be used to. This isn't merely a resting place for the dead. For magic never truly dies. This is a place where bodies rest, while magic wanders free."

His eyes went to the cemetery, focusing on something in the distance, past the gates. I followed his gaze, watching as the mist didn't just move around the tombstones, but took on various familiar shapes as well. The shape of a woman with long hair rose up from the mist like a cresting wave. Her face contorted into a silent scream. And then another wave washed over her, carrying her away.

I shuddered.

"No one will think less of you if you change your mind and would like to go back now," Ethelwulf said, his voice but a whisper.

I considered staying outside those gates. But there was one very good reason that couldn't keep me from going in there for anything.

"My mother is in there, isn't she?"

Gran had said she was cremated, but there was something about the way she'd said it and the way she'd refused to say any more on the subject that I never understood. Until now.

"Yes, but—" the elf started.

"I'm going in. That's all there is to it. "

"Melantha—" Rhiannon started.

"I'm going in."

"This isn't solely a place where lawful magical beings rest," Ethelwulf said. "No one is turned away. There simply isn't anywhere else for them to go."

I heard the slight emphasis on "lawful".

"So there's black magic users in there?" I asked.

"And worse," Paul muttered, as though he was trying to keep from being heard.

I'd forgotten about the "worse". Now that I'd been reminded, I wasn't so keen on running into the roaming spirits of the "worse". Maybe seeing my mother's grave could wait. Maybe missing Paul's ceremony wasn't such a big deal.

"I will look out for her," Rhiannon volunteered. "You should be at home resting," she said to Ethelwulf.

"Perhaps I should, but this must come first, and I wouldn't miss it for the world."

Hobbling on his cane, he led our meagre group up to the iron gates, and tapped with the handle of his cane.

"I am glad you decided to join us," he said to her, while we waited.

"After that speech you made about learning from our mistakes?" She shrugged. "I guess, like you, I wouldn't miss this either."

"You mean it?" Paul said, turning on Ethelwulf's shoulder.

"I miss Vincent. The Vincent I knew before he fell in with that gang," she said softly. "He wouldn't want me to hate you. The Vincent I knew was forgiving. He wouldn't like to see us fighting."

"He loved you," Paul said softly. "Even after he went bad."

She smiled. "Thanks."

The gates groaned as they unlatched and separated from each other, sounding as though they'd not been moved in a thousand years and as if moving now was a great and terrible chore. The groaning steadily rose in pitch as the gates crept open, the sound becoming a high-pitched squeal that was so unbearable I clamped my hands over my ears. I thought my head was about to burst. Then all was silent.

I slowly dropped my hands, hoping the noise was over. I still felt uneasy, so I folded my arms over my chest, hugging myself tight.

"There's just one thing you need to know about the cemetery," Ethelwulf said. "Don't touch the mist of wandering magic."

"Why not? What would happen?"

"The mist will take your magic by severing what ever part of your body comes into contact with it."

I shuddered and pulled my sweater tighter.

We trod along the gravel path, our steps making crunching sounds. The sky had grown considerably darker since we'd arrived at the cemetery. It was colder, too, under the shadows of the tall evergreen trees. I wished I had my jacket.

As soon as we passed the gates, the mist parted, revealing a clear path, and as we moved deeper into the cemetery, and the gates closed on their own, the mist wrapped around behind us, leaving our group to stroll the cemetery in a mist-free bubble, like a spotlight in a dark room.

The path led us around tombstones of various designs and ages, all set haphazardly among gnarled leafless trees. The ground-hugging mist concealed everything in the cemetery from about my knees down. It was impossible to guess at the number of graves. I could only see the tallest of the tombstones. I strained my eyes, trying to read every name as we marched past. It was a task that had me feeling like I was being swallowed by quicksand. It could take years to read every gravestone. And that was just the ones above the mist. If this was like any normal cemetery, there were older markers flat on the ground. But with the mist growing steadily thicker with every step deeper into the cemetery, the prospect of reading every name became more and more of an impossibility.

I had the distinct feeling the cemetery had secrets it intended to keep hidden.

We made our way along the path, into the heart of the cemetery.

Several robed figures became visible. So did their weapons.

I breathed in a sharp gasp. My feet came to a halt. They were the same dark hooded figures that I saw at Ethelwulf's apartment, but each of them now carried a sword or a double-headed axe, or a scythe. Each instrument was polished to a high silvery shine.

Rhiannon's fingers wrapped around my arm.

"Keep moving," she whispered. "Don't let them see your fear."

Why not? What would happen? I would have asked her about it, but we'd reached the ring of Elders.

A deep voice boomed, "You've brought among you Paulinus Gennarus Magnus the Third."

It was a statement, not a question, but Ethelwulf stepped forward and replied, "Yes, Elder. We have."

"What is the purpose of the remainder of your group?"

"We come today in support of Paulinus," the elf replied in a strong voice. He was of similar height to the Elders, but he seemed small by comparison. Their presence was bigger. They seemed larger than the rest of us, larger than life, somehow.

"All of you?"

I suddenly felt as if I was being x-rayed. I couldn't see or feel the rays seeking answers from within, but I knew they were there. Somehow the Elders were inside my mind, poking at my intentions, searching for a weakness. I focused my thoughts on Paul and the good I knew of him.

"Yes," Rhiannon said boldly, as she released my arm and stepped in front of me. "Even I am here in support of Paulinus."

"Rhiannon Barbardina Broom. Even you."

It wasn't a statement; it wasn't a question. A challenge.

The voice continued, "You say you are here to support Paulinus, but you have doubt. Speak the truth. Speak your heart."

Her shoulders sagged. "The truth— The truth is . . . I'm here in support of Paulinus's brother, Vincent."

I froze. Shocked by her sudden betrayal. She'd said she was here to support Paul. What the hell was she doing?

"You are not aligned with the purpose of this ceremony. You shall be cast out—"

"Wait," Paul shouted.

"Paulinus. You have something to say on this matter?" The voice sounded curious. But it also sounded like it was unheard of to interrupt an Elder, let alone to argue for keeping someone who didn't support you.

"You asked for the truth," Paul said. "She spoke the truth. She deserves to stay for that alone, but what's more is I know her heart is with Vincent. Mine is as well." He paused for a deep breath. "The truth is Rhiannon is the closest thing I have to family. I would like her to stay."

"Her doubt will leave you vulnerable to the negative energy, to the spirits of the worst kind. She will be the weak link. Are you certain you want to risk your outcome?"

"Uh—" Paul hesitated. He crawled around on Ethelwulf's shoulder, turning so he could face Rhiannon. His antennae dropped. The choice weighed heavily on him.

"It's okay, Paul," she said softly. "I understand. I'll go."

Ethelwulf, until now, had observed the exchange between Paul and the Elders with a pained expression. Now he looked positively desolate.

Rhiannon turned to leave, also appearing saddened by this development. I think she wanted to support Paul, but she didn't know how to without betraying Vincent.

"Wait," I found myself saying. "I trust her. She's never let Ethelwulf down. She's taken good care of me. She's fought hard for justice for us all. I want her to stay."

Paul and Rhiannon both seemed relieved. Ethelwulf frowned, worried.

"What do you know of the matter?" the voice asked.

"They're my friends," I said softly.

"Are you certain you want Rhiannon Barbardina Broom present?" the voice asked, but it wasn't talking to me. "We will not ask again."

"I trust her with my life," Paul said.

For a time, no one said anything. Maybe the Elders were waiting for Paul to back down, to agree with them and send Rhiannon away.

Finally, the booming Elder spoke again. I wondered if he had any other volume.

"The decision has been made," he said, but exactly what had been decided wasn't clear. I waited.

I thought for sure they were going to cast out Rhiannon. Risking Paul to the bad spirits sounded like a bad idea. Much worse than offending Rhiannon.

Instead, they made an opening in their circle.

Ethelwulf hobbled past them to a big stone table. He held out his palm, where Paul sat twitching his antennae.

"Hop down," the elf said softly, but Paul didn't move. He swivelled his eyes to look up at Ethelwulf.

"It'll be all right," the elf said, but there was an edge to his voice. For once, I wasn't sure I believed him.

Paul heard the edge in Ethelwulf's voice, too. The elf angled his hand, encouraging the cricket slide off. On trembling legs, Paul crawled away from the comfort of his friend to the cold hard table.

If a cricket could look worried, then Paul certainly did. Not that I blamed him. I'd be worried too, if I was surrounded by dark robed figures holding sharp weapons, and there was a potential negative energy leak.

The Elders turned and left a gap in their circle, which the three of us filled. Then they started talking in a language I'd never heard. It wasn't quite talking, but more like chanting. I stopped trying to make out the words and listened to the rhythm. Until something else caught my attention.

While the Elders chanted, the mist swirled as if moved by a light breeze. But I felt no such wind. The mist took on shapes of humans and other creatures. But they were no longer silent. The mist whispered.

"— such a shame—"

"— terrible what will happen—"

"— death before life—"

"— beautiful sacrifice—"

"— at long last—"

So many voices spoke at once, I couldn't follow a single one. I caught only a few words between the chanting. But it was enough. An image of what was going to happen began to form in my mind. And it gave me the chills.

Were these the evil spirits? Could I warn the Elders? Would I get us into trouble if I did? What would happen if the ceremony was interrupted right now?

The chanting rose in pitch and volume, becoming as intense and frightening as the sight of their weapons rising over their heads, ready to strike.

They weren't going to hurt Paul, were they? I remembered the Elders' words, The decision has been made, and those from the mist, beautiful sacrifice.

Paul was trembling so much— he had to be terrified. Ethelwulf and Rhiannon looked worried.

And then the unimaginable happened: the swords, the axes, the scythes, were all brought swiftly forward, slicing the air— headed straight for Paul.

"No!" I cried. I lunged. Rhiannon caught my arm, but too late.

It all happened so fast, and yet as if in slow motion.

The Elder next to me turned out his hand, fingers spread wide. In a flash of light, everything froze. The noise, the weapons, Rhiannon— everything and everyone was frozen in time.

Except for the Elder next to me. He lifted his sword, turning it toward me. The very tip— the very sharp tip— came to a halt pressing up just under my chin.

CHAPTER NINETEEN

THE FACE INSIDE the dark hood was so ancient it was no more than a skin-wrapped skull. His nose was sunken into the hollows of his face. His eyes held the ferocity of a lion defending a fresh carcass from a pack of hyenas.

"What do we have here?" he asked. His voice was so deep it vibrated through my rib cage.

Oh, great. They were going to cast me out.

"Are you going to kill Paul?" My voice was weak and fell dead in the mist. I tried not to look at the Elders who were all frozen in mid-strike. I shuddered.

His eyes were void of eyelashes. His whole head was hairless. It was unsettling.

He narrowed his eyes. He tsked. "An almost-turner. What does an almost-turner know about life and death?"

The challenge was not just in his voice. It was in the way he adjusted his grip on the sword. It was in the air, sharp and electric. Maybe he intended it to be a rhetorical question. Maybe this was an interrogation.

"Paul is my friend."

As soon as I said it, I realized it was true. Paul was the best friend I'd ever had.

"Friendship is dangerous," the Elder said.

"My Gran says the same thing."

"But you don't believe it."

"I don't understand it."

"You will soon enough."

I didn't like the sound of that. "Do you mean Savion? He's in trouble.

Why won't you let us help him?"

Maybe I should have been afraid of this Elder, but I wasn't. I didn't feel he meant me harm. It was more like he had a message for me.

"The one you call Savion can't be helped."

"Why not? I don't understand."

"If removed from his father, will his life get better or worse?"

"Why are you asking me? Isn't that a question I should be asking you?" I was pretty sure Ethelwulf was going to find out what might happen if Savion was separated from his father, but in the meantime all we had was speculation.

The skin on his forehead wrinkled. If he'd had eyebrows, he would have just raised them.

If he wanted me to discuss how my life had changed since my mother died, then he would be waiting a good long time.

"That's a question for Savion," I said. "So if you let me go rescue him, you can ask him yourself."

The Elder opened his mouth and erupted with a dark clatter that made my toes curl. It took me a moment to realize he was laughing at me.

I immediately wanted to take it back. Being flippant with Gran was one thing, but with an Elder . . . What had I been thinking? I wanted to crawl into a hole and die.

"Why?" he asked.

"Why save Savion?" I asked. What a dumb question. "Because his father is slowly killing him."

"Why is he worth saving?"

Again, I didn't understand him. "All life is worth saving."

"Is it?"

If I'd been given a choice of having a philosophical debate with an ogre or with this Elder, I would have chosen the ogre. At least it was only visually disturbing to hear grandiose ideas coming from an ogre. From the Elder, it was not only upsetting to look at him, but he was making my brain hurt.

The Elder seemed to be suggesting some lives weren't worth saving. I didn't know if that's what he was implying or not, but I didn't like it one bit. I had to believe all lives were worth something to someone.

A small part of me decided to agree with the Elder.

Even murderers? that small part of me asked. Are the lives of murderers worth saving?

I shook my head. "I'm not qualified to take part in this debate. But if there's one thing I know for certain, I know my Gran is worth saving. Not debatable."

He stared at me. My heart hammered in my throat. What was I thinking? I just sassed an Elder. How stupid was that? When was I going to learn to keep my mouth shut?

"I have forbidden you to go."

And I'll probably go anyway. Though I didn't say it, I thought it. Gran had forbidden me to take this mission and I went anyway.

A small part of me wondered if Gran had been right.

He laughed again, but then quickly sobered.

"You believe Paulinus's life is in danger from us?" he asked.

I blinked. It took me a moment to absorb the change in conversation. If you could call this a conversation.

"Isn't it?" I asked. Was this a trick question?

"Your uncertainty is your greatest weakness. You need to learn faith, child of Lavinia. You need to learn when to put the needs of others before your own selfish needs, grandchild of Alberta. The tasks set before you will be your test. If you fail, we will meet again. There will be no second chance."

He didn't give me a chance to respond. He turned to Ethelwulf, and opened his mouth. All sound was drowned out by a high-pitched scream and its twin— an earth-trembling roar. I saw the sharp weapons crash down on Paul before a blinding light washed out all sight. I stumbled backwards, crashing into Rhiannon, with my eyes squeezed shut against the light. I fell to the ground, my hands covering my ears to block the sound.

The noise died away. I could smell the sharp tang of copper and sulphur in the air. I opened my eyes to see the Elders form a tight ring around the table, excluding the three of us. I thought I heard them whispering, but it was hard to tell with the ringing in my ears.

Rhiannon helped me to my feet. She looked scared. She stood next to me, wide-eyed, and wringing her hands.

They didn't seem to know time had been frozen. Which meant they didn't know about my conversation with the Elder. But now was not the time to fill them in.

Ethelwulf put on a brave face, and then nudged his way into the ring. They let him through, swallowing him up between their dark robes.

"Is Paul—" I started to say, but Rhiannon held a finger to her lips to silence me. I stretched up on tip-toes, trying to see over the shoulders of the Elders.

"Well," Ethelwulf said, "there's a sight you don't see every day."

"Hey . . ." came a weak voice. Was it Paul? Chills ran over my skin. Was he alive? What had the Elders done to him?

I heard wheezing and coughing. A raspy voice said, "I'd forgotten what it was like to have lungs."

Lungs . . . Crickets breathed by taking air into their air sacs via their spiracles. Thank you, biology class. Did that mean the procedure had worked?

I looked to Rhiannon for some kind of confirmation. She chewed her lip, straining for a glimpse of what was going on inside that ring.

I'd never seen her look so worried. It seemed so completely at odds with her short hair. Maybe her confidence was washed away with the pink she removed from her hair. Or maybe, despite her reservations about him and his magic, she did care about Paul.

I heard more coughing, but it disappeared under a deep hum that seemed to be coming from the Elders. It grew in volume. The vibration sent goose bumps over my skin. An orange glow rose up from the centre of the ring of Elders, shining like the setting sun.

I'd thought they were done. What's happening?

The hum and glow swelled, growing louder, more intense. Then it became chanting, until the glow burst open, spreading multi-coloured rays of light in all directions. It was like a disco ball of power.

My own blood swelled, drawn to the surface until it hovered just under the skin, as if it had been pulled there by a magnet. My breath took up the rhythm of chant, and I found myself mouthing words I didn't know. My senses overloaded with the intensity of it all. As the multi-coloured rays died away, I was left with the taste of burnt copper in my mouth.

I didn't wait this time. Before Rhiannon could stop me, I pushed between the Elders, ignoring the feel of jutting bones under the dark, rough wool.

I caught a glimpse of a human on the table.

"Paul!" I called out. The Elders tried to hold me back.

"Mel?" It sounded like Paul, though his voice was groggy. It was also richer, deeper and more human. "Where are you?"

The Elders succeeded in keeping me out of their circle. Pressing their shoulders tight, they formed an impenetrable barrier. I might have been able to see over their shoulders if I was taller.

"I'm here," I said. I sagged back to my feet. He sounded alone. Frightened. And I couldn't get to him. "Are you okay?"

Emotion swelled at the back of my throat. He was alive. Alive.

"I think . . ." he said, "all my parts seem to be here." He sounded relieved. "Wait— What's this? What did you people do? Oh, no! You got it all wrong!"

Ethelwulf tried to get Paul to calm down, but the restored wizard was lost in his own outrage. The Elders mumbled responses, surprised to hear there was a problem. There was so much talking at once, I couldn't make out what anyone was saying, except for Paul.

"Look at me!" he shouted. "I've never looked like this. You've turned me into someone else. I'm ginger! And freckled!"

"He's fine," I heard one of the Elders say.

"Yes, perfectly," said another.

They turned and filed out of the ceremonial area, trekking down the gravel path. Finally, I was able to get near the new Paul. I just wasn't sure I wanted to.

"Wait!" Paul shouted. "Come back! You can't leave me like this! I'm naked!"

"Here," Rhiannon said. She removed her scarf and held it open. It was a wide scarf, wide enough to be used as a skirt.

The new Paul was a redhead with fair, ruddy skin and billion pale freckles. He frowned at the scarf.

"I'm not worried about my neck," he said.

"Wrap it around your waist like a skirt," she said.

He gave her a look. "I don't wear skirts."

"Then think of it like a kilt." She hid a smile. She was enjoying this.

"Hmph."

"I didn't have to offer it to you." She seemed offended, but I thought she was rather still playing with him.

Paul snatched it from her and began wrapping it around his hips.

Ethelwulf clapped him on the shoulder. "It's nice to have you back, old friend."

Given the way these two had carried on, I'd been expecting Paul to be an old man. Not a young man of about Rhiannon's age.

"This isn't me," Paul protested. "I don't look like this. Why would they do this?"

"It's a good look for you," Ethelwulf said, trying to hide a smile. "I'm sure that must be it."

Paul grumbled.

"I don't get it," I said. "What's the big deal?"

"I'm all red. And spotted!"

"So?"

"So— Oh, forget it." He hopped off the table and adjusted his scarf skirt. He wobbled on his new legs and had to grab the table to keep from falling over. "This is going to take some getting used to."

"No kidding," Rhiannon said. She turned and headed for the main gate. She was bitter again. I thought the fight was over. I thought they were going to try to be friends again.

Paul took one step in her direction and fell down.

"Well, this is embarrassing," he said, using the table to pull himself up. He wobbled like a newborn calf.

"You'll get it figured out," Ethelwulf said, leaning on his cane. He hobbled over to Paul and offered his arm.

Paul looked at him. "Is this like the blind leading the blind?"

The elf laughed. "You'll be as good as new before I will."

"About that," I said, coming around to Paul's other side before he brought the two of them to the ground. "If they can do all this, why can't they restore your powers?"

"Thanks," Paul said, giving me a smile as he accepted my help. "You know, you look different from up here."

I smiled. "Duh. You're a full head and shoulders taller than me now." I looked over at Ethelwulf. "You were saying?"

"Ah, well." He cleared his throat.

"What he's saying," Paul said, "is that he gave up having his powers restored so I could have mine back."

"But you'll get yours back?" I asked.

"When the Elders have refreshed, yes," Ethelwulf answered. "I'll have to endure a few rounds of what Paul just went through."

"Wow. That energy bomb must have been pretty powerful."

"Oh, make no mistake. Lebrun is extremely knowledgeable. It's part of what makes him so dangerous. His bomb seared my cells in such a way that they must heal before they will hold or generate magic again."

Before long we were back on the cobblestone streets, and Paul was walking semi-normally.

Ethelwulf stopped when we reached the main street.

"And now, my friends, we part. You have much work to do," he said.

"We do?" Paul and I said in unison.

Ethelwulf clucked his tongue. "The sorcerer is not going to catch himself, is he?"

"The mission was cancelled."

"The mission has changed," Ethelwulf said firmly.

"This can wait until you're well again," Paul said quietly.

"You must retrieve Alberta."

"But the risks—"

"We are all well aware of the risks, Paul."

"But I haven't used magic in years. What if I fail?"

"I trust you, Paul," the elf said, giving the younger man a pointed look.

"I know you do." He bowed his head, eyes downcast.

"What you need now is to trust yourself. What I need now is to rest."

We took Ethelwulf back to his place, and then began preparations.

CHAPTER TWENTY

THE CHOICE WAS simple: we could spend several hours driving to the Lebruns' cottage, or we could alacroport and get there in seconds. There were only two options. But the choice was not easy for me.

The Three Ps had done their homework. They'd traced Gerrard's income tax filings and registered properties and found the cottage on the south side of Algonquin Park. They'd called up a real estate agent and learned it was a three-story house on 300 acres fronting the Madawaska River.

Horatia had been in charge of packing the supplies. I had no idea what she'd packed. I don't think any of us had any idea what we would do once we got there. I'd had to borrow clothing from Rhiannon.

Knocking on the front door wasn't going to work. Getting Savion to let us in wasn't going to work, either. Not after last time. We knew Gerrard employed warning systems and took security precautions, so sneaking in also wasn't going to be an option.

"So what exactly is our plan?" I asked and yawned as I slipped into the jacket Rhiannon had loaned me. We were gathered back in Rhiannon's apartment, preparing to leave before the sun was even up.

Horatia snorted. "Isn't it obvious? We don't have one!" She cackled.

"What do you mean we don't have one?" I wasn't quite awake. Maybe I'd misheard her.

Rhiannon gave me a sympathetic smile. "Our first task is to get in. Beyond that . . ." She shrugged. "Get Alberta, maybe Savion, and get out."

"I know that, but how are we getting in undetected? Do we have cloaking devices or something?"

She smiled. "Wouldn't that be nice? Sadly, no. You're our best hope for getting in."

"Me?" I shook my head. "After last time, Savion is not going to let me in."

"We are hopeful Lebrun's warning charms are only looking for turners, elves, and magic users, that they aren't so finely tuned to look for almost-turners as well."

Oh boy. Our plan rested entirely on me. Again.

"And if he has accounted for almost-turners?"

She frowned. "I really doubt he has. The house in Ottawa wasn't guarded against almost-turners, and when we last saw him, he wasn't in any shape to tune a radio station, let alone protection charms."

Either she was right, or I was going to end up injured. Or dead.

"But what if he's feeling better?" I asked. "The first thing I would do is fortify my defenses so I could heal in peace."

"Savion is not yet a spell-turner. Gerrard is not going to tune a charm that will constantly battle his son. Once Savion gains his powers, Gerrard can tune the charm to exclude the two of them, and maybe then the charm will include almost-turners."

Maybe she had a point, and maybe she didn't. Gerrard's watch didn't glow when he first arrived home. It didn't glow until Ethelwulf and his team arrived. Maybe it excluded himself and almost-turners. Maybe it didn't. We didn't have enough data to work with. We'd just have to wait and see.

I was also troubled by the proximity of my birthday. Maybe it made a difference. Maybe it didn't.

Then there was the matter of the conversation with the Elder. What was the test? That he'd forbidden me to go and I went anyway? Or was it something else? What would happen if I didn't pass the test? Would they execute me?

My breakfast formed a hard, bitter lump in my stomach. I forced myself to stop thinking about it all and just concentrate on one moment at a time.

Horatia and Rhiannon discussed the various possible securities Gerrard might have employed. Paul threw his few cents in, but he was brand-new to the case as much as I was. The Three Ps elaborated on the layout of the property and buildings.

I stopped listening after hearing about "fire sentries". I caught Paul's eyes. I wasn't equipped to counter-charm any of this— with or without Council powers. And we both knew it.

Charms. Spells. Magic. What good was any of it in a world so full of evil? Once we had Gerrard, there would be someone else to chase, to capture, to fear. That's why this rag-tag group existed: to capture those who used their magic to hurt others.

The problem nobody was addressing was magic. When humans hurt humans, doctors could help. When magic was involved . . . there was no going back. Even Ethelwulf admitted there was no way to fix a magical being. Poor Thorn. He would never walk again. How he must hate magic right now.

It was time to alacroport.

"I don't know about this," I said to Paul as soon as I could get him away from the others. A nervous worry had taken up residence in my stomach.

"What do you mean? You can't back out now, Mel. This mission was your idea." He stuffed a shirt into his backpack.

The others zipped their bags shut and strapped them on. They supposedly carried everything we would need between them. I had my doubts.

I swallowed, pushing down the fear. "I haven't— you know..."

"What?" he asked, not looking up from his packing.

"Paul." He stopped what he was doing. My eyes pleaded with him to understand. To get it, so I wouldn't have to say it in front of the others.

"Oh," he said. "You haven't used magic before."

The whole room stopped what they were doing.

"Thanks," I muttered.

A huge grin spread across his face. "Come on, Mel. When have I ever kept quiet about anything?"

Rhiannon was more sympathetic. "We already know you haven't used real magic before. You haven't had it. You have almost-turner powers."

"The old fox gave her a little something extra," Paul said, still grinning.

Glad he found this so amusing. I didn't.

"Ethelwulf gave you Council powers and didn't teach you how to use them? Didn't test them?" Horatia blurted. "Merlin's mercy!"

"We don't have time for this," Rhiannon stated.

"You go ahead," Paul said. He'd dropped the grin, though his eyes still shone with amusement. "I'll run through the basics with her."

"You? A banished turner?" Rhiannon snorted.

"Formerly banished," Paul corrected stiffly. "I'm still a blood turner, therefore I'm not only the best one for the job, but I happen to be the one Ethelwulf picked for the job."

I rolled my eyes. "You can both shut up because I don't plan on using Council's powers. So somebody alacroport me so we can get his over with."

Suddenly all sets of eyes in the room were on me. They all started talking at once, demanding to know how I was going to capture Gerrard if I didn't plan on using Council's powers.

"Whoa!" I waited until they shut up. "My part in this is to let you guys in, open the door, extend the invitation, so you can you do your Council duty and rescue Gran."

The room was silent as they mulled that over. I hoped I was making the right decision. A tiny nagging feeling told me I might actually need Council's powers— that Ethelwulf might have given them to me for a reason— but I ignored that feeling. Using magic only lead to people dying.

"You'll still need to learn to alacroport," Rhiannon said.

"Doesn't the Sanctuary have a door that will open near the cottage?" I asked hopefully.

"Why on earth would it?" Horatia blatantly stated. "His cottage is not a hub of activity for turners, you know. He doesn't use the Sanctuary, anyway, so why would there be a door?"

I shrugged. It was just a thought.

"You brought me to the Sanctuary, Rhiannon. Won't you take me to the cottage?"

They all fidgeted in silence, seeming to not want to tell me yet again that I needed to learn the spell for myself.

"The alacroport is a simple spell, Mel," Paul said.

Anything to make them go away. "Fine. But nothing else."

While the others alacroported to our destination, Paul turned to me with a grin. "This is going to be fun, sweetcakes."

Obviously Paul and I had different ideas of fun.

Paul explained the basics to me. Something about thinking about where you're going and feeling yourself moving from this place to that place while turning the spell. I was only half listening. I was more interested in the fact Rhiannon hadn't left yet.

"Okay, so now let's give it a shot," Paul said full of enthusiasm.

"I don't think so," Rhiannon interjected. "You haven't told her about the atoms."

"What atoms?" I asked. I should have known to keep my mouth shut.

Paul tensed. "I was saving that for later," he said, his voice strained as if he was trying to convey some hidden meaning in his words.

"Paul, she needs to know so she can turn the spell properly."

"She can find out later. If she's a blood turner, it won't matter."

"If she's not, it will," Rhiannon argued.

"What atoms? What are you talking about?" I demanded.

"Nothing," Paul said too quickly.

Rhiannon rolled her eyes. "Magic doesn't just evolve out of the air," she said.

"Yes, it does," Paul argued.

Rhiannon blinked, but otherwise ignored him. "When you alacroport, you have to disassemble your body atom-by-atom, move it, and then rebuild it," she finished.

"Sounds complicated." I hated the spell already. And yet was completely fascinated by it.

"Don't listen to her, Mel," Paul said, stepping between me and Rhiannon so I couldn't see her. "You don't need to know that. Let's just get started."

"Paul, you can't just skip the science like it doesn't exist," Rhiannon insisted.

"Watch me, sister," he retorted and then turned back to me. "We're going to practice with—" He glanced around the apartment. "This pair of shoes." He scooped a pair of Rhiannon's purple Doc Martens off the floor and held them up triumphantly. Then he placed them before me with a hand gesture like a magician doing a big reveal.

Rhiannon gasped. "What! You can't do this with shoes, Paul!" she scolded.

"If you don't like my teaching methods, Rhiannon, then don't stay to watch!" he fired back.

She huffed. "I'm not leaving you here to kill somebody or destroy my apartment!"

"Then shut up and let me work!" he said. "All she has to do is work the alacroport spell on the shoes. Then she can try it on herself."

"That doesn't make any sense!"

While they continued to argue about how and what they were going to teach me, I started to put together everything they said. Magic hovered under my skin. It was always there, even when I didn't want it to be. Sometimes just talking about magic caused it to wake and swirl. It coiled inside of me, begging to be let out. So with all this talk of taking apart atoms, thinking about the destination and putting atoms back together, I felt the alacroport spell forming, ready to be turned.

So I did it.

I focused my mind on Rhiannon's purple shoes, thinking about them, where they were, how they were made, what they were made of, right down to the tiny atoms. Then I turned the spell, feeling it leave my fingertips, and stretch out to take the atoms apart one-by-one. Though I started to sweat from the exertion, pulling apart the atoms was relatively easy. Putting it all back together, now that was a different story.

I should have planned out where I was going to alacroport the shoes. Deciding at the last second, mid-spell, was probably a bad idea. The best I could think of was to send them across to the other side of the room to the floor beside the couch. Using magic as a basket, I envisioned scooping up the atoms and carrying them across the room, where they were reassembled into their original shape. By Rhiannon's and Paul's accounts of the spell, it should have worked.

I wasn't expecting the atoms to interlock so quickly.

It was all I could do to hold the magic together long enough to get it over the couch. I barely got the stream of atoms where I wanted them, when they slammed together. Faster and faster, they crashed into each other like strong magnets. Each collision made a small bang, and as more collisions happened, the bangs grew louder and louder.

It wasn't a crack or boom like Ethelwulf's alacroport. This sounded more like a box of firecrackers going off.

At the sound of the first snap, crackle and pop, Paul and Rhiannon jumped back, taking shelter behind furniture. When the noise finally stopped and all was quiet, they cautiously peered out from behind their makeshift blast shields.

I was afraid to look.

The result was a misshapen blob of purple leather, as though Rhiannon's Docs were made of clay and giant hands had squished them.

Rhiannon gasped. "My shoes!"

"I'm sorry," I said hurriedly. "I'll buy you a new pair."

She didn't reply. She shook her head and picked up her backpack. When she looked at me, there was something a lot like fear in her eyes. She gave Paul a look that distinctly said "I told you so." Then she alacroported out of there.

I'd expected Paul to laugh at my failure, to tease me about my lack of control. He didn't. He would barely look at me.

"I really screwed up, didn't I?" I could hardly get the words out. The disappointment in the room was suffocating.

"Oh, Rhiannon's just sore 'cause I was right," he said, but there was a heaviness to his words, a sense of dread weighing on his shoulders.

"You told her I would screw up?" I didn't remember hearing that. In fact, I couldn't remember the two of them having a private conversation.

"You didn't screw up, Mel," Paul said. He sounded almost angry. "That was the best darn first-time alacroport spell we've ever seen, and you didn't need a focus to do it."

"What does that mean?" I asked. There was something he wasn't telling me.

"It means, you'll definitely be a blood magic turner," he said.

Chills broke out on my arms. "Is that a bad thing?"

"It's not the best thing, but it's not the worst either."

I believed him, and I knew he was telling me the truth. But I still felt there was more that wasn't being said. "Then why are you two so mad at me?"

"We're not mad," he said.

He took my hand and alacroported us together to the rendez-vous location.

Again Paul hadn't told a lie. Without words, he'd told me the truth: they weren't mad; they were scared. They were scared of me.

CHAPTER TWENTY-ONE

WE ALACROPORTED FROM the Sanctuary to a spot down the road from from the Lebrun acreage. We were assigned tasks as soon as we arrived. Paul and I were going to walk around the south perimeter of the Lebrun residence, Rhiannon had already headed for the north side, the Three Ps were helping Horatia set up our headquarters. We would make our attempt to get onto the property in the evening.

I felt the pull of magic right away.

The last theory the group discussed back at Rhiannon's apartment was one that suggested if Lebrun had used the filthiest of black magic to guard his Ottawa house, then his cottage might not be so bad. The cottage was farther away and more difficult to maintain while he was in Ottawa, and that much I understood, but I still had questions. As we set about on our reconnoitre, I asked Paul about this "theory".

"All magic draws from nature," he said. The sky had lightened to an inky blue in the morning twilight. The clouds parted from the horizon like a heavy curtain. Here, in the shadows of the trees, it was cold and dark. We picked our way around pine trees, cedar clumps and rocky ledges. The snow squeaked and crunched under our feet, sounding as though we walked on Styrofoam. Technically, we were trespassing on other people's properties. I had asked about that, but nobody thought it would be a problem.

"There certainly is plenty of nature out here," I muttered.

Paul snorted. "No kidding. But most of it's not Lebrun's type, so finding a weak spot shouldn't be a problem."

Unlike in the city where his house was surrounded by a neighbourhood full of exactly his type: walking sacks of blood, otherwise known as people. Out here, the closest neighbour was easily a couple of kilometres away.

Still, something about this theory nagged at me.

And it was more than just the mysterious feeling of being pulled along by an invisible thread.

"It's not by coincidence that we're on this case, is it?" I asked.

"Are you kidding? With that old fox at the helm?" Paul grinned, but he wasn't quite back to his jovial self.

While I was sure Ethelwulf was to blame, there was something more to me and Paul being on this case.

"Magic is passed down maternally. I should be a white turner like my mother and Gran. Why am I not?"

Paul glanced at me before pushing branches out of his way.

"Are you asking me to explain biology?" he asked.

He was dodging me by answering with questions. There was something he didn't want to tell me.

I had to ask.

"Are we related?" I asked. It was a simple yes or no question. He couldn't get out of it.

"Don't we all go back to Adam and Eve? Or the cave dude that evolved from a lizard?" he asked.

"Paul. Why can't you just answer the question?"

"Oh, lots of reasons." He sounded annoyed.

"Paul! I thought you were my friend. Why can't you just tell me?"

"Because I don't think you're really asking if you and I are related. And I don't like what you're implying. And how the hell should I know, anyway? I've been neutralized for the last twenty years!"

"Twenty years? Really?" I was surprised. He appeared to be in his early twenties, same as Rhiannon. If he was really in his twenties, how could he have been married? And in an archaic arranged marriage at that? But if he had been neutralized twenty years ago, then it seemed unlikely we were related. Maybe.

"Really. Twenty years," he grumbled.

I gathered it was going to be a while before Rhiannon got over Paul being himself again. She'd had twenty years to blame him for Vincent's death.

"How old are you?" I asked. I knew turners lived longer than average humans.

"Almost two hundred years old," he said quietly.

Two hundred? That was going back a lot farther than I thought. I wondered how old Gerrard was. How old was Ethelwulf? And Gran? How old had my mother been when she died?

"So are we related or aren't we?" I asked. If he was as old as he said he was, it was possible. "What are you not telling me, Paul?"

The tension in the mysterious thread of magic had tightened as we'd hiked deeper into the woods. It hummed under my skin like an intense feeling like I'd forgotten something. Something really really important.

"Nothing. It's just a story."

He clenched his teeth and adjusted his jacket like he was uncomfortable. I wondered if he felt the weird pull, too.

"What story?" I asked.

It was like he was fighting with himself about telling me or not. Finally, his shoulders sagged. "Blood magic isn't passed down from turner to turner."

"What are you saying?" Clearly I was my mother's daughter, so what was he getting at?

"Blood magic chooses the turner." His voice was soft, apologetic.

I was sure I misheard him. I had to have misheard him.

"Wait," I said. I grabbed his arm to make him stop for a moment. "Say that again."

He repeated it, and I knew he spoke the truth by the painful expression in his eyes. He didn't want to tell me. He could see how much this news upset me. He was sorry he had to be the one to tell me.

"How is that possible?" I asked. My voice had gone soft. It was all I could do to remain standing on my trembling legs. Magic picked turners? Really, it bore repeating: magic picked turners? Magic picked? It was like suggesting sunshine sang opera. To say magic chose anything was to suggest a degree of thought was involved. How could magic think? Magic was energy. It wasn't alive.

I definitely didn't like the suggestion that magic had somehow chosen Gerrard Lebrun and made him a blood turner. What purpose could magic possibly have to do that?

And then there was the idea that magic had picked me. For what purpose? Why was I deemed so worthy? I didn't want anything to do with magic. It didn't work for me. I couldn't even turn an alacroport spell.

"The universe is about balance, Mel," Paul said. "If turners can choose to follow black magic, then magic can choose the turner. When something dies, something new is born. Balance."

"So it's all random choices," I said.

"I don't know about that," Paul said. "I've always been told that everything happens for a reason."

I'd always been told that too, but so far, for everything that'd happened in my life, I wasn't seeing any good reasons.

The breeze shifted and I caught a whiff of something I really wished I hadn't.

"Wait," I said. We were surrounded by ice-covered rocks and stark birch trees. But something was different. "Do you feel that?"

I could hear water rushing nearby. We were near the river that bordered the east side of the property. A chill wind blew from the river, bringing damp and the scent of rot.

"Ugh. No, but I smell it," Paul said, clearly disgusted. Also, clearly hiding something. He felt it. He just didn't want to say so.

I tucked my mouth and nose into my jacket. "What is that?"

Paul mumbled something I didn't hear, taking tentative steps in the deceptively deep snow. He didn't make a move to cover his face, in fact when the breeze blew, he tipped his chin into it and sniffed. After no more than twenty steps, he stopped again. I didn't have to ask why.

The property was surrounded by an ancient farm fence of rusted wires strung from post to post. It was a fence meant more for keeping cattle in than for keeping people out. At only a metre and a half high, it would be an easy climb.

Up ahead, a large prone form lay rotting next to the fence, its dark brown fur completely covered in blood.

I turned my eyes away from the gash across the bull moose's throat and belly where its insides spilled out across the snow.

"That's disgusting," I said, fighting the urge to vomit.

"That's a sacrifice," Paul said quietly.

"Sacrifice? Sacrifice for what?" My mind reeling, trying to erase the image of so much blood.

Paul's one word answer was enough to give me chills.

"Reinforcement."

CHAPTER TWENTY-TWO

PAUL DIDN'T HAVE to explain. His urgent pace and sombre mood was more than enough to tell me we were in trouble. Although, the moose was kind of a dead giveaway.

By the time we'd returned to headquarters, the indigo shadows had shrunk, retreating from the brightening sky. The sun was up, but it failed to bring any warmth to this February day.

"Where'd the others go?" I asked, stopping abruptly under the trees. Paul marched on ahead, through the ditch and to the road.

"There," he said, pointing.

"I don't see anything." All I saw were tall pine trees interspersed among cedars and junipers.

Paul grinned. "They did a great job, didn't they?"

"Huh. Brilliant." I still didn't know what he saw, but I saw a whole lot of nothing.

"Come on," Paul urged, crossing the road. "Horatia should have breakfast and bunks ready."

"Bunks? Where?"

Ignoring my questions, Paul jumped from the road, over the snow, and into the ditch. He stepped through tracks that could have been left by a deer, and slipped under the feathery branches of a huge pine tree.

I followed Paul. Something felt weird about the snow, and I realized our feet weren't leaving tracks. At least, not boot-prints. Behind us, all that remained were the tiny tracks of deer.

Crouching down so I could fit under the tree, I pushed back the pine boughs and stepped into a warm kitchen.

Horatia stood in front of a camp stove propped up next to the tree trunk— a trunk that was somehow several meters wide, and yet, not.

I glanced over my shoulder at the sun rising through the forest on the other side of the road, and back at the room before me where the Three Ps sat on a wood-framed chesterfield. They were watching cartoons on a TV. Horatia hummed a squeaky tune as she stirred a pot of what smelled like chili.

Paul stamped his feet, knocking the snow off his boots.

"Is chili for breakfast a turner thing I don't know about?" I asked him.

"It's a Horatia thing," he replied. Then he tromped up three short stairs that disappeared into the evergreen branches to my right. Across the room, an identical set went up on my left.

"Close the door, you're letting in a draught!" she cackled at me.

"But—" It was all so Alice in Wonderland.

"Oh, come on, now. It's not the first time you've seen magic."

I let the branch fall behind me with the curious sensation of closing the flap of a canvas tent.

"Boys, time to set the table," she commanded. I stayed where I was, marvelling at how we'd somehow become tiny and I hadn't felt a thing. Maybe tiny wasn't right. I shuffled my boots around on the snow and dirt floor. Our boot prints appeared normal sized. The walls were made of snow. The roof was the tree itself, the limbs criss-crossed overhead like timber beams in a large house.

The scent of spicy chili and warm air brought my eyes back to rest on the large pot on the stove. Where had all that stuff come from? She'd only brought a simple trunk with her. The oven door squeaked as Horatia pulled out a pan of freshly baked rolls.

The Three Ps picked up the chesterfield, turned it upside-down, and suddenly it was a long picnic table with benches.

"Huh." Magic.

"Brr," said a voice behind me. Rhiannon dusted snow off her legs and shook off her long scarf. "Well done, Horatia," she said, taking in the room with approval.

"I smell breakfast," Paul said, descending the stairs.

"Let's eat," Horatia said, sitting at the table. The Three Ps took up one whole bench by themselves. I had no choice but to sit between Paul and Rhiannon. My stomach wasn't quite ready for chili for breakfast, so I nibbled on the roll.

This feud of theirs was going to be a problem, I just knew it. No matter how much they denied it. How could we present a united front against Lebrun if they couldn't stop bickering? I opened my mouth to start a dialogue and hopefully get it dealt with, but Paul started talking about the dead moose.

"I found a stag on the north side just as you so thoughtfully described in excruciating detail," Rhiannon said. She put her down her spoon and pushed her bowl of chili away.

Paul saw the gesture and frowned. "Sorry, but we need to change our plans."

"It doesn't change anything, Paulinus," she argued. "We expected him to put up defenses."

"It's Paul. And you're wrong. We expected him to use what little defenses he relied on while he lived in the city. We did not expect him to have enough strength to go out and hunt down a sacrifice, let alone two."

"I don't know why you didn't expect it. He's an evil sorcerer the likes of which we've never seen! What else would he do?"

"He could have more. He could have a whole herd of cattle on his property. He could be using them to regain his powers."

I felt my eyes widen. A fierce cold gripped my insides.

"Can he do that? Use cows?" I asked. We hadn't thought of that. Why hadn't we thought of that?

"Horrors!" Horatia cried. "What will we do now?"

Across the table, the Three Ps had observed the conversation in silence, turning their heads simultaneously to look from one speaker to then the next. Now they turned their eyes on me.

"We proceed," they said in unison. "Just as planned. We will use the girl to disable the security and let us in."

"Me?" I said weakly.

They tipped their heads, peering at me. "Despite appearances, you are not of age. Therefore, you are not a turner, not a magical being. Magical security systems will not affect you."

They were creeping me out. I liked them better when they were quiet.

"I don't know anything about turning off magical security systems," I said.

"There is no 'off'," they said. At the same time, they put their spoons into their bowls of chili. "Once inside, you will invite us in as before."

I guessed they didn't know Ethelwulf left that part out when he gave me the plan for the last mission. He'd just showed up. I had no idea I was to invite him in.

As before. They made it all sound so simple. We'd had Ethelwulf before. They had approval from the Elders before. I was only remotely involved before.

"Mother Mabel's mustard molasses," Horatia said, dropping her face into her hands. "We're doomed!"

"It could work," Rhiannon said, sounding more hopeful than she looked.

"It will work," Paul corrected. "She did it before. She'll do it again."

So it was decided.

I wished Ethelwulf was here.

***

After our meal— not quite breakfast, not quite brunch— Horatia handed each of us a handkerchief and sent us off to bed, while she cleaned up and packed everything away in a trunk. I followed Rhiannon up the stairs to the left. We were to rest, so we could set the plan in motion in the late afternoon, toward dusk. It was decided the darkness would give us better cover.

The stairs led to a small room with walls covered in pine panelling. Floorboards creaked with every step. It was all so bizarre. I was fascinated as Rhiannon unfolded the handkerchief and shook it out. It flipped open and turned itself into a cot and sleeping bag. I couldn't help but feel a thrill of joy when my handkerchief did the same.

I'd brought my backpack with a few overnight essentials that Rhiannon had given me— toothbrush, hairbrush, pyjamas. As I pulled them out of the bag and went through the motions of getting ready for bed, I felt a stab of loss, of homesickness. As nice as this place was, as nice as the Sanctuary was, I'd rather have been in my own bed, in my own apartment, even if it was just me and Gran.

I cleared my throat to swallow down the sob I was trying to hide, and sniffed. I shouldn't have bothered. I felt more than saw Rhiannon stiffen, but I knew well enough now that nothing escaped her.

She didn't ask what was bothering me. She didn't say anything until I was changed and sitting on my bunk, staring into space.

She sat beside me on the cot and said, "Sometimes I wish Ethelwulf would think things through before he pulled people into our crusade."

I knew she was speaking about me, but it sounded like there had been others.

She continued, "This is a little before my time with the Council, but there were some who didn't want your mother involved. They didn't think a woman with a child should put herself in such a dangerous position. They thought someone single, younger should do the job."

"You?" I guessed.

She sighed. "Ethelwulf said their reasons were exactly why Lavinia was perfect for the job. No one would expect such a move by the Council."

"That's what my mom and Gran fought about, I guess. And why Gran didn't want me taking this job. I understand now why my mom was gone several months of the year. She was in the Sanctuary, wasn't she? Working undercover?"

She nodded.

"But it was cruel to not let me have friends. Gran should never have held me prisoner."

Rhiannon inclined her head. "Maybe."

"What do you mean 'maybe'? You agree with her?"

"How old were you when your father died? Seven? Eight?"

An icy stillness seized my chest, and then was blown apart by the rapid beating of my heart and the rise of anger.

"What does this have to do with my father?" I didn't like the sound of where this was going.

"What do you remember of him?"

"My father was a good person." I couldn't help it. I was angry. I wasn't entirely sure why, but I was angry. "I hope you're not suggesting otherwise."

I sounded threatening, and I didn't care if she thought it was an empty threat or not. Finding out my mother was living a double life was bad enough. I wasn't about to accept such surprises about my father.

"I'm sorry," she said. "I didn't know him very well. And what I've heard may not be accurate. I was hoping you could fill in some of the blanks."

That's what she said, but what she meant was she didn't want to let slip more than I'd already been told.

Which meant there were surprises about my father.

"You met my father?"

She nodded. "Just once. It was at a winter solstice party."

I sighed. "He was a math professor at the University of Ottawa. He died the day before my eighth birthday."

She nodded. "He was in the hospital a lot."

I twisted my mouth into a frown. "He had haemophilia."

"A disease that required frequent blood transfusions."

Everything inside me went still.

I was a blood turner . . . Gerrard Lebrun was a blood turner . . . and a doctor.

Rhiannon picked at her fingernails, her hands on her knees, her head bowed so I couldn't see her face.

"Did you ever meet his doctor?" she asked quietly.

I didn't trust myself to speak. All I could do was shake my head.

"Your father was referred to a world-renowned haematologist. Someone your parents believed would help them."

"Gerrard Lebrun." I didn't remember it. I didn't know the name of my father's doctor. I'd never met him. I was just making a guess.

A guess I didn't like, didn't want to be true.

"They believed Lebrun was working on a cure. We all believed it," Rhiannon said softly.

I shook my head. It was too much. Too much.

"He killed my father?" I asked. I couldn't put it together, and yet it fit. Why hadn't I made the connection before?

"He killed a lot of people," Rhiannon said. "They all believed he was helping them."

"But— why? Why is he doing this?" I asked.

"The rumour we've heard is he was trying to study your father's blood condition and use it to take magic out of turners."

"How?"

"From what we've heard, he believed the inability to form blood clots could be used to prevent magic from binding to the turner. That is, once a turner was given a transfusion of blood from a haemophiliac, Lebrun believed the magic would flow right out of the turner."

"Why? Why is he sucking the magic out of us? Why is he doing this?"

Rhiannon sighed. "Several years ago, a turner accidentally killed his wife."

"So he's out for revenge?"

I rubbed my face, muttering 'no', but the surprises weren't going away.

"Why are you telling me this?" I asked.

"You need to know who we're facing, what we're up against. He's not just powerful. He's blinded by his delusions, his warped view of the world. He truly believes what he is doing is good."

I shook my head. "I mean, why are you telling me this now?"

Here we were about to attack an insane sorcerer, while we had him cornered, and he held hostages, and it all hinged on me, a powerless almost-turner.

"I'm getting to that. You know magic requires belief in it to work, right?" she said, and I nodded. "And that magic is neither good nor evil, but is a tool that has neither a minimum nor maximum power requirement?"

"Yeah, yeah," I said. "Magic doesn't kill people. People kill people."

"Oh, no. Magic kills people," she said. "You wanted to know what was worse than black magic."

I remembered asking. I wasn't so sure I wanted to know the answer anymore.

She continued, "What's worse is when one man's good intentions are turned against him in a quest for more power. Turned by magic. To fulfill a power requirement that knows no maximum."

"Are you saying Gerrard doesn't control his magic, that it controls him?"

Was such a thing even possible?

"It scarcely ever happens, but it does happen." She shuddered. "We believe magic has used Lebrun's grief to turn him against us."

"But why would magic want to do that?"

"The magic that Lebrun successfully takes from turners doesn't just disappear. It's absorbed into him. It's making him more powerful. Revenge is just magic's excuse to get Lebrun to do what it wants."

"So, if I'm understanding right, then Gerrard isn't the monster. He's the monster's creator."

She considered. "More Jekyll and Hyde than Frankenstein. Lebrun is still the monster."

"Then I don't get it," I said.

"Lebrun started out using black magic, but now the magic uses him, too. It whispers to him. And he chooses to listen to it."

"That sounds like an excuse for his unacceptable behaviour," I said.

"I'm telling you this so you know the truth. So you understand what we have to do," Rhiannon said.

"Meaning kill him."

"There may be no other way," she said. "He is too far gone with black magic. We might not be able to contain him."

"You mean control him. Like you did with Paul."

She sighed. "Paul—"

"Is a good person, Rhiannon. Whatever he did before, whatever he was like back then, he's changed. He's helpful, he's kind, he's considerate."

"Maybe with you."

"With everyone."

She was quiet for a time. After a while she said, "You think I'm being too hard on him."

It was my turn to sigh. I agreed; she was being too hard on him, but there was more to it than that, and I would have to choose my words carefully. "I think maybe you're judging him based on the person he used to be, and not on the person he is now. He's learned, he's grown, and he cares about you."

Horatia came up the stairs then, carrying a tray of mugs. It smelled like hot chocolate. Rhiannon got up and went to her own bunk.

"A little something to help you sleep, dear," the old woman said, handing me a mug.

Like there was any way I was going to sleep now. My mind was a windstorm of thoughts. And I thought I had something to worry about before.

The hot chocolate was warm and smooth and delicious. It filled the hollow in my belly. I knew from the moment it was handed to me that it was loaded with a sleeping potion, but I drank it anyway. I snuggled into my sleeping bag that was the perfect temperature— not too hot, not too cold. I hoped my dreams wouldn't be filled with pictures of insane haematologists pumping blood into innocent turners.

I was sure Rhiannon thought she was doing the right thing by telling me about what happened to my father and the magic inside Gerrard, but I was also sure her timing could have been better.

As waves of potion-induced exhaustion threatened to pull me under, I heard the women whisper on the other side of the room.

"Did you tell her the truth?" Horatia asked.

"I told her enough." Rhiannon didn't sound as relieved as she should have.

The older woman grunted. "You should have told her it all."

"She has enough to deal with."

"She's been kept in the dark for too long."

I thought they'd stopped talking, maybe drifted off to sleep, but then I heard Rhiannon reply.

"She's a smart girl. She'll know what to do."

CHAPTER TWENTY-THREE

As a group, we retraced the path Paul and I had hiked earlier that morning, but we weren't going all the way to the stream and the moose carcass. We went about halfway along the property, and then confronted the fence.

"Why are we doing this here and not at the gate?" I asked.

"The gate's too obvious," Paul said. "We like a challenge."

He earned himself a sharp look from Rhiannon.

"It's too exposed," she said. "We could be discovered at the gate. We're much less likely to be discovered here."

"The gate is locked, " Horatia added.

"Don't you guys have an unlock spell or something?"

Horatia snorted. "That's the first thing any good turner guards against with a protection spell."

Great.

I looked at the fence. It was just a simple construction of wire attached to wood posts. But it stood before me as vast and impenetrable as the walls of a fortress.

"Mel—" Paul started.

"Save it," I interrupted. "I know what you're going to say. It's going to be all right, blah, blah, blah."

He raised a ruddy eyebrow at me, and he put on an expression I'd come to know as his "challenging" expression. Strangely, it was not much unlike when he would quirk an antennae at me.

"Actually," Paul said, "all I wanted to tell you was that your boot lace is undone."

I scowled at him, not sure I wanted to believe him. He laughed. I had to admit I felt disappointed. Didn't he want to give me a pep talk? Was he lying to make me look at my boots so he could laugh at me? To say he made me look? It would be like Paul to try to lighten the mood by joking around. Paul the cricket definitely would tell me my lace was undone just to make me look. But Paul the turner— or was it Paul the wizard?— was different, and I wasn't sure how to take him anymore.

Paul quirked an eyebrow at me again, as if daring me to look at my boots.

He shrugged. "It's your boot lace."

Rhiannon clucked her tongue and sighed, clearly thinking we were being childish. The Three Ps were silent pillars. I could always count on Horatia for the blunt truth.

"Just tie it already and get on with this!" Horatia scolded.

Rhiannon put her hand on my shoulder. "I know you're nervous. Try to relax. Remember, you just have to let us into the house, and we'll take care of the rest."

"I'm not nervous," I said, but nobody believed it. Not even me.

I pulled my mittens off and retied my boot. Paul tried to hide a smirk. Badly.

"Are we finished with the theatrics?" Rhiannon asked.

I took a deep breath. "Let's do this."

I approached the fence. Earlier, I'd felt the hum of a thread of energy, but now I felt nothing. Even with my mittens off, and my hands held within inches of the wires, I sensed nothing.

"What do you feel?" Horatia asked. She stood next to me, also with her hands hovering over the wires. A little further down next to her, Rhiannon did the same.

"Nothing," I said.

"Nothing?" she said. "How can that be? There has to be magic thrumming through these wires."

Rhiannon the metal turner agreed. "The metal should be alive with magic, yet I sense only the wire."

Even Paul didn't sense anything from the fence. "The blood magic couldn't have worn off already, could it?"

"Shouldn't you know?" I asked, shocked. "You're the blood turner!"

He had the grace to turn red with embarrassment. "It's been a while, okay?" He turned his nose up with indignation. "Besides, I'm a wizard."

The other turners roll their eyes at Paul's statement. The Three Ps were behind me, so I couldn't see their reaction, but I had a feeling they didn't exactly believe in this wizard stuff either.

"So how are we going to figure out if there's magical guards in the fence or not?" I asked.

"Touch it," Horatia said. Again, I could always count on her to get straight to the point.

I didn't want to touch it. No way. Rhiannon could see it in my eyes. She opened her mouth to speak, but I cut her off.

"Yeah, I know," I said. "Don't be nervous, I just have to let you guys into the house, blah, blah, blah."

Really, I was getting tired of their pep talks. The fact was, none of them had to go first or alone anywhere. They worked together in prime numbers. The capture of Gerrard rested on me. Again. My mother always said "everything happens for a reason". Paul told me blood magic chooses the turner. The Elder said this mission would be a test. Did that mean I'd been chosen to be the one to capture Gerrard?

"Actually," Rhiannon said, "I was going to say I wouldn't want to touch it either. This is a heavy responsibility for someone your age. You should be at home doing homework and worrying about boys. I'm sorry you were dragged into this."

I appreciated her words, though they changed nothing. "I still have to be the one to touch it, though, don't I?"

"Mel," Paul said, picking up on my irritation. He laid an arm across my shoulder. "You don't have to do this."

"What are you doing, Paulinus?" Horatia demanded.

"Yeah, I do," I said.

"No, you don't," he insisted. "You can walk away right now."

"No, she can't!" Horatia cried. "She's the one! She's the only one who can let us in!"

"We'll find another way," Paul snapped at her.

"Paul, you can't tell Melantha to quit now," Rhiannon said.

"You said yourself you wouldn't want to do this, Rhiannon," Paul scolded. "We can't force her to do something we wouldn't do ourselves."

All the hope, concern and expectation in Rhiannon's face fell. Her shoulders sagged. "You're right. You don't have to do this, Melantha."

"What are you fools doing?" Horatia cried, throwing up her hands. "We can't do this without the girl!"

"But she shouldn't be the one to test the fence," Paul said with resolve. His arm fell away from my shoulders and he turned toward the wires.

"Paul, what are you doing?" I asked.

"I will test the fence," he said. "If it's good, I'll lift you over."

"If it's not?" I asked.

He shifted his jaw.

"If it's not, he will die!" Horatia blurted.

Paul appeared to be unhappy with the situation, but determined to do whatever it took.

But what if they were right and the fence was warded to keep out turners and elves, but allow almost-turners? Paul could be hurt or killed by the protection spell. And given the dead moose and deer, it was going to be a powerful spell.

But neither did I want to test the fence. I didn't want to get hurt. Or die.

Paul took a deep breath, squared his shoulders and reached out.

In that split second, with every fiber of my being, I knew I couldn't let him touch it first. I knew without a doubt it had to be me. It was why I was here.

Without thinking, I grabbed the fence wire. Just a hair before Paul did.

I don't know what I was expecting to happen, but I wasn't expecting nothing. Which is what happened: nothing.

Paul and I looked at each other. He burst out laughing.

"Last one over the fence is a rotten egg!" he dared, stepping onto the wires and throwing his leg over. I did the same, with less grace than Paul, but I made it over, landing in the soft snow on the other side.

All that build-up, all that worry, and for nothing. I couldn't stop grinning. I made it! The fence wasn't guarded after all!

Paul was helping Horatia when things went wrong. Paul held most of her weight on our side of the fence, but her feet were still perched on the wire from the other side.

Exactly what happened, I couldn't tell you. I didn't notice anything change. I only knew there was a problem when Horatia started screaming.

"Throw me back," she cried between breaths.

That's when we saw the blood. Dark red drops fell into the snow, seeping through her white quilted jacket on both sides. It looked like someone had tried to cut her in half inside her coat.

"But—" Paul grunted. He didn't move. Maybe he was weighing the options. Would throwing her back stop the spell or make it worse?

She screamed louder. She looked like she was going to pass out.

"Just do it," I shouted. Everyone seemed to be too stunned to think.

Paul blinked. Maybe he couldn't move. Maybe she was too heavy. Or maybe he was just in shock. I didn't know and I didn't wait to find out.

I lunged forward and shoved. I'm by no means strong enough to lift someone of Horatia's size and girth, but my shove was enough to knock her off balance. She fell back, into the arms of the others on the other side.

She stopped screaming. Maybe from the blood loss or the intensity of the pain. It didn't matter which. The damage had been done.

While Paul and I watched helplessly, Rhiannon went straight to work on stopping the bleeding.

The Three Ps turned their heads toward us. "You must go," they said.

Rhiannon looked up, alarmed. "We can't let them go alone. They're both—"

She didn't need to finish that thought. We knew what she meant.

We were the only two blood turners. And the guard spell had let us pass.

It had been a bad idea to send us. Now it just seemed down right stupid. Dangerous. Having only us inside was insane.

The Three Ps continued in chorus, "But go they must. If they remain here, they will be captured. The alarm has been activated." One of the Three Ps poked at the fence with his cane. The tip reached the space between the wires, but would not pass through. He pushed harder. It still would not go.

"I invite you in," I said.

But the cane would not pass through. I repeated, but still it would not go. Electric sparks shot out around the cane. When he pulled it away, clouds of smoke drifted from the tip.

"What am I doing wrong?" I asked, feeling desperate.

"Nothing," the Three Ps said. "This is a new shield. We cannot come in this way. Find out what you can about the house. Meet us as the gate. If the shield is at all vulnerable, that will be the spot."

"But he might see us at the gate."

"It is a risk. Go. We will tend to Horatia and then meet you there."

"We should abort," Paul said, his face as white as the snow at our feet.

Rhiannon was inclined to agree.

"We can't," I said hurriedly. "They're right. The alarm has been sounded. If we quit now, Gerrard will run. And he'll be a whole lot stronger when we find him next."

The wind ruffled the treetops high above our heads. The river gushed in the background. Somewhere in the distance a wolf howled. Except for Horatia's laboured breathing, the others were silent.

The mission had become hopeless. We were without Ethelwulf, Thorn and the goat. Now we were down by one more. And two turners who could be used to Gerrard's advantage were the only two on the inside.

"There's no way for us to get back over the fence now," I whispered.

Rhiannon's slumped shoulders indicated her answer. She wouldn't look at us.

"Go," the Three Ps said with finality.

Paul took my hand and we turned to leave.

"Know this," the Three Ps said. "This shield was not set by magic wielded by spell-turners or elves, but by a creature brutal in both heart and strength despite its limited size. You must defeat it before we will be able to enter the property. It is the keeper of these grounds."

"What is it?" I asked, not liking the sound of anything described as brutal in both heart and strength.

Paul's single word answer fell heavy with dread in the midnight shadows of the dark forest.

"Dwarf."

CHAPTER TWENTY-FOUR

"WHAT DO THEY mean by brutal?" I asked in a low voice once we were on our way.

The others were carrying Horatia back to camp. Since she'd been injured by magic, they didn't want to risk using magic to get back to the tent. They had no choice but to carry her until they could heal her enough to alacroport out of here.

I wished we could have gone with them. I wished we were storming this castle all together.

I wasn't sorry to leave behind the crimson snow. On the other hand, I wasn't looking forward to whatever was out there waiting for us. I needed to know more about what we were up against. So I asked.

Paul had been muttering under his breath as he picked his way through the trees, trying to lay a path that would keep us in the shadows, and away from the open areas. Though dark now, an orange full moon crested the horizon and soon would reflect enough light on the snow to rival a cloudy day. He stopped and turned to me, the lines across his forehead tightly drawn, indicating his worries.

"You saw what happened at the fence," Paul said. It was a statement, but there was a hint of a question in his voice, as though he was wondering why I even had to ask. I guess I didn't. The brutality had been obvious.

"But that magic—" I tried again. The image of Horatia on that fence was forever burned in my mind. "It was like it wasn't even there, and then suddenly it was. They can hide their magic, can't they?"

"Yeah, I guess they can," he answered.

"What else can dwarves do?"

Paul frowned. "I don't have first-hand experience with dwarves. I didn't know they even existed. You're asking the wrong person."

"But you've heard stories?" I guessed. He'd heard something. I could tell. He just didn't want to admit it.

"Stories." He snorted. "More like nightmares. What I remember of them would put human horror movies to shame."

He wouldn't say any more, and I wasn't sure I wanted to hear more anyway. I never liked horror movies.

Paul was different now that he was a spell-turner. I kind of missed Paul the cricket. He was more fun. Then again, the changes in Paul had started once Rhiannon was in the picture. And now that I thought about it, she'd changed too. Rhiannon was different from the light-hearted, pink-haired turner I'd first met. Her changes started when she learned of Paul.

They were both darker, more bitter, and my Gran would say they argued like an old married couple.

Paul was muttering again. I decided we both needed a distraction.

"You should ask Rhiannon out," I said. "You two would make a cute couple."

He snorted. "Are you crazy? She hates my guts."

"I've seen the way she looks at you. That's not hate in her eyes."

He faltered then, stumbling on a large rock. I was right. They did used to be a couple.

"You already dated her before," I pressed. "So what's the big deal? Ask her out again."

"We never dated," he said shortly.

"But—"

"We were married."

"What?"

We stopped next to a grove of cedar trees. The open glade we'd worked our way around glittered in the moonlight.

"We were young, it was an arranged marriage, and she was in love with my brother, Vincent," he said, spurting out bitter tones. "Whatever you think you see in her eyes, you're wrong. How can she not hate the man who made his vows to her, broke them, and then killed the one she loved?"

Married. For the life of me I didn't expect that. Dated, yes. Married, never.

Yes, it had to suck to be in love with someone but stuck in an arranged marriage. Not having met Vincent, I didn't know what she had loved about him, but there was nothing unlikeable about Paul. Annoying, yes. But being forced to marry him couldn't have been that bad. I told him as much.

"Look," he said, "I wasn't kind to her back then. I wasn't stupid; I knew she wanted to be with Vincent. But she was with me and I never let her forget it."

"Paul—"

"Mel, I've been trying to start over. I'm not the same person I was back then. She has every right to hate me, and every right to never let me forget it."

He resumed our approach to the house, and by my estimates, we were close. I wouldn't get another chance to talk to him about this. Maybe never. The distraction worked, though. He'd let go of some of his fear, only to hang on to his sorrow. I wondered if I'd done the right thing. If he would be focused enough to fight whatever we were about to encounter.

I was right about one thing, though. It wasn't hate I saw in Rhiannon's eyes. It was regret. Whatever hatred she'd had for him, she'd let go. Yet she seemed to be still punishing him, but that wasn't because she didn't care.

If Rhiannon could get past their past, maybe they had a chance at a future.

"What about you?" Paul asked. "Tell me about this boy. Rory."

"Rory? What about him?"

He grinned. "Now who's evading questions with more questions?"

"I learned from the best," I said, returning his grin.

"Uh huh. So, Rory. He asked you to go steady?"

"Wow. How old are you again? Nobody says 'go steady' anymore."

Paul laughed. "Okay, nicely evaded again, young grasshopper. But you are 'dating', 'hanging', 'chillin'?"

"Chillin'?" I couldn't believe he just said that.

"Spill it, Mel," Paul demanded in a friendly tone, but I could tell his patience were growing thin.

"Okay. Yes, he's my boyfriend. Are you happy now?" I couldn't help but throw some irritation at him. He should have known. He was there in his box in my backpack. I reminded him.

"Yeah," he said. "I just wanted to hear you say it."

I huffed like a drama queen and gave him a playful shove.

"You make a cute couple, Mel," Paul said.

At that happy thought, I followed Paul with a smile on my face.

As it turns out, it was my last happy thought of the day.

***

The trees tree trunks grew more narrow, spread farther apart. Paul made me wait alone while he scouted for a better vantage point. We were nearly to the house, and had failed to run into the dwarf-thing, whatever it was. I was feeling pretty good about our chances of getting to the front gate and then getting into the house.

Until Paul returned and changed everything.

"Shit," he panted, crouching next to me. We were behind a cluster of bushy cedar trees.

I'd never heard Paul swear before.

"He's old," he said. "Not good."

"Who?"

"The dwarf."

"Did he see you?"

Paul shook his head. "But he's protecting the house."

"How do we defeat him?" I asked, remembering what the Three Ps said. Why didn't they tell us how to defeat him?

"Not sure." He shook his head again and swallowed. "I don't remember."

I gave him a look.

"What? I was never very good at staying awake during the old stories." He shrugged.

"We have no weapons," I said, pointing out the obvious.

Paul turned to me with a smile and some of his old devilish self shining through. "I have an idea, sweetcakes."

He told me what he had in mind.

"Are you crazy?" I whispered harshly.

He waved at me to keep quiet. We were crouched next to a garden shed that sat at the outer edge of the back yard. From here we could see the entire back of the house. It was a big house. It couldn't have been more than a few years old. The style was modern, the materials were trendy and expensive, and there was very little landscaping. The trees in the yard were mere saplings. Where the house in the city had a lived-in, homey feeling, this house felt stoic, sterile and empty.

"You got a better plan?" Paul challenged.

"No, but this is suicidal, Paul."

He gave me a look that told me he already knew that, and he didn't appreciate hearing it.

"Just do your part, sweetcakes, and I'll do mine." He tried to smile, but it didn't quite work.

"Paul . . ." I begged. His kamikaze idea was to distract the dwarf while I grabbed a shovel from the shed, then used it to whack the dwarf on the head and knock it out. The dwarf would then drop its shields and the others could come in and help us get rid of it and get inside the house. Presto.

I was worried about Paul. He'd grown less cheerful and more depressed every day since getting reacquainted with Rhiannon. Here he was throwing himself at the mercy of a brutal creature and it sounded like he didn't care what the outcome was.

Call me paranoid.

He saw my expression and tried to cheer me up. "Hey, if I can go up against a high school full of teenagers in sneakers and winter boots as a cricket, then I think I can take on a puny dwarf as all this." He gestured at his new body.

"All this?"

He smiled. "Now get a shovel and get ready."

And before I could summon another word, he took off. He pranced across the thick layer of snow covering the yard. He scooped up a handful of snow, which he packed into a hard ball and lobbed at the house. I flinched, anticipating shattered glass, but it never reached its target.

The snowball got within a meter of the building and splattered. Broken chunks of snow slid down an invisible barrier.

That confirmed one thing: I wouldn't be able to get into the house until we'd dealt with the dwarf.

While Paul juggled with three snowballs, I examined the house. The windows were dark— blinds shut, curtains closed. Some windows had a faint light around the edges where the blinds didn't quite reach. But the windows with the bright lights were the short basement windows.

"Who the hell are you?" A loud, sharp voice brought my attention back to Paul.

The creature was no more than half a meter tall with a snow white beard, blue tunic, and tall red hat. A garden gnome.

This was the brutal dwarf?

Paul caught the three snowballs and shrugged, a sheepish grin on his face. "Frosty the snowman?"

I choked on a laugh, watching helplessly as the harmless little old garden gnome pulled out a heavy hammer and a mining pick— right out of nowhere— and charged after Paul.

I stared in horror as Paul stood there, too stunned to move. The dwarf ran with a speed I wouldn't have thought possible for such short legs. I couldn't shout, couldn't call out to Paul to tell him to get the hell out of there. The plan hinged on me sneaking into the shed undetected.

But I couldn't just let that dwarf hurt Paul. I had to do something.

Just as I opened my mouth to yell, Paul broke free from his shock and pelted the dwarf with the snowballs, then took off running. Paul chugged his arms and pounced over the snow. The dwarf easily deflected the snowballs with its pickaxe.

I would have sighed with relief if it wasn't so intense.

While Paul ran around the yard with an angry dwarf chasing after him — the pair resembling a scene out of a cartoon— I slipped into the garden shed.

I could still hear Paul's wails as I navigated the earthy darkness, searching for two things: a rope and something to use as a weapon. Paul wanted a shovel. I would have taken anything, but fortunately, I had several shovels to choose from. I settled on the one closest to me, a heavy flat one with a square bottom.

Rope, on the other hand— that was the challenge. There was a couple of balls of twine inside a terra cotta pot. But I had to figure the dwarf could probably break through simple twine. Subduing the dwarf was going to be hard enough. Keeping him out of the way for the next several hours, now that was going to be the trick. If I didn't find rope, I didn't know what we would do to keep him out of the way.

Trying to see into the shed using only moonlight reflected on snow was next to impossible, but thankfully, someone liked to be organized. Everything was so neat and tidy, I had no problem finding anything. Except rope. There wasn't any to be found in the little shed.

Maybe I didn't need rope. There was lots of electrical cords. Several long ones hung from pegs in neat bundles. I grabbed a fat bundle of orange cord.

Expect the unexpected. I guessed that was the lesson of the day.

As I edged toward the door, I realized I could no longer hear Paul charging through the crunchy snow bellowing his head off. I only heard the sound of my own breathing.

Paul.

What happened? He was supposed to be loud to help cover my noise in the shed. So why wasn't he making any sound?

Then I heard something. It wasn't footsteps. It sounded more like— chopping.

I slipped the bundle of cord over my arm, grabbed the shovel, and took off running through the snow.

I rounded the corner to the front yard, and there, next to the driveway was the worst thing imaginable. The dwarf stood over Paul, the pickaxe raised over his head, ready to strike. Paul rolled out of the way, but the dwarf attacked again with the hammer in his other hand. Again Paul rolled, and again the dwarf struck. Again and again and again.

Worse, Paul was bleeding.

CHAPTER TWENTY-FIVE

GARDENING WAS NEVER a pastime of my mother's. She preferred reading to most everything. My father's time in the outdoors amounted to little more than cutting the grass every week. So to be here, up against a gnome wielding a pickaxe in one hand and ball-peen hammer in the other, with only a shovel and electrical cord in defence, was an entirely new experience for me.

He was such a small creature— barely a half-meter, and that included the hat. He was so cute in that tiny blue tunic and shoes that curled up at the toes. Who would have thought something so cute could be so vicious? Or have such excellent hearing?

He heard me coming. I ran at him ready to whack him with the shovel, but he swung his heavy hammer around in time. The clash vibrated in my hands, and sent waves of shock up my arms. I almost dropped the shovel. I almost didn't get it up in time to ward off another blow from the pickaxe.

"Hey!" I shouted. "Watch what you're doing!"

Had I stopped to think about it, I might have realized what I was doing was suicidal, and if I'd realized that, I wouldn't have found myself staring into tiny eyes narrowed with anger.

I did the first thing that came to mind: I ran.

Running through deep snow was just like running through the ocean: slow, slogging hard work. Wanting to put as much distance between me and the dwarf, I chose to go down the shoveled driveway, away from the house rather than through the thigh-deep snow in the yard. But what was an easier path for me was also an easier path for the dwarf. He caught up to me in no time.

Faced with the iron-gate before me and dense woods on both sides, there was nowhere to go. So I prepared to fight.

I whirled around, swinging the shovel at his height. The shovel found its mark on his face. He flew back, hitting the packed snow with a hard thump. He raised his tools to defend himself, but I wasn't aiming for him. I swung the shovel and knocked the axe out of his hand. It arched through the air and landed in a snow bank. I went for the hammer next, but he caught on. He took the hammer in both hands and swung at me. It hit the shovel with a loud clang that vibrated up both my arms and rattled my teeth.

When he whacked again, I wasn't prepared. The shovel went flying. It hit a tree and fell into deep snow.

The dwarf grinned, revealing sharp, pointed teeth. "Trespassers will be prosecuted."

"Bring it." I'd been shoved around by Gerrard Lebrun. Was I really going to worry about this little pint-sized garden gnome?

. . .brutal in both heart and strength . . .

Yeah, probably I should..

He charged for me. I jumped over him, but screwed up the landing. I slipped on a patch of ice. Pain shot through my ankle. I hit the cold ground, barely remembering to roll. I reached out with both hands just in time to grab his hammer arm before he hit my face.

"Trespassers will be shot on sight," he said, leaning on the hammer.

The Ps were right. He did have incredible strength. I couldn't hold him back. My arms trembled, weakening. He was too strong. It took everything I had to roll and direct the hammer to the ground where my chest had been a heartbeat before.

I shoved him with my good foot. I ignored the pain in my ankle, and climbed to a standing position.

"What next?" I asked. "Beware of dog? Oh, that would be you."

I threw the extension cord aside.

"You really need a hammer to fight a mortal girl?" I challenged. "Wow. You must have serious weaknesses to compensate for."

It was a stupid thing to say. I saw the change on his face. He understood what I'd said. But mouthing off at him worked. He dropped the hammer and made a trajectory for my face. I caught him, just as he sunk claws into my cheeks, and we both tumbled to the ground. I rolled, trying to pin him. But he was stronger than I'd anticipated.

The hits came fast. Faster than I could react. What had I done? This damn thing was going to kill me. That was his job. And I'd just taunted him into doing it.

I managed to get my arms up to shield my face from the worst of the blows. But it didn't stop him. He simply worked on trying to break my arms and get his small fists around my thin bones to the softer parts of my face.

How was I going to get out of this?

And suddenly, I didn't have to worry about it. The dwarf was off me. Paul was yelling my name, but through a thick fog of pain and a bone deep ache.

What damn thing is he yelling about now? Can't he see I'm in pain?

"— gate! Mel! You've got to open the gate!"

I knew he was talking to me. I even knew what he wanted me to do. I just didn't know how to make my body move through the screaming pain.

"Please, Mel!"

Something in his voice ultimately made me move. Something primal, desperate and full of fear. It was a sound I didn't like coming from him. It was a sound I would do anything to never hear again. Including getting my sorry butt off the snow and to the gate.

I didn't dare look back until I'd lifted the latch. Rhiannon and the Three Ps were waiting there and the looks on their faces confirmed as much. The gate slid open, but they couldn't enter until we'd finished with the dwarf. With renewed energy, I raced back to Paul.

He was in trouble. He had the dwarf captured under his right arm like a football. His left hand made circles as he looped the extension cord around the body of the evil creature.

That was the good part. The bad part. . . The creature had sunk its teeth into Paul's side, biting into his ribs through his parka. It gnawed, chewed, bit and tore into my friend's flesh. Paul fell to his knees.

I took the cord from his trembling hand and looped it around the dwarf's head, pulling tighter and tighter until it opened its jaws and released Paul. Quickly I threw another loop, catching the cord in the dwarf's mouth. I looped again and again until it was bound and gagged.

It refused to recognize defeat. It worked on chewing its way through the cord. It bucked and writhed on the ground until it was up on its pointed toe slippers once more. And then it charged at me, bouncing, head-butting my legs.

"Hey," I said, between breaths. "Enough. You lost."

I took a step back. It hopped up to me and head butted me again.

"Stop that." I took another step back. It followed.

"Stop it or I'll— I'll steal your hat!" I snapped. It was a stupid, idle threat. What else did a dwarf have any how?

But the threat meant something to the dwarf. It blinked.

"Wait a minute. . ." I muttered, forming a picture. "I'll take your hat," I said, testing a theory. "I will."

The dwarf started hopping away from me. I glanced at Paul. He was in rough shape, barely conscious. He held both hands on his bleeding side. But he'd heard me. He nodded.

I took two strides and snatched the hat off the dwarf's head. The air crackled like a room full of Christmas crackers snapping apart. Blue and red sparkles chased each other from the ground up the length of the extension cord, around and around the dwarf, until they came off the top with a bang, and the dwarf was turned to stone.

"Huh," was all I could manage to say.

The others, Rhiannon and the Three Ps, joined us. The solidifying of the dwarf meant the end of the guard spells. Paul went slack.

"Paul!" Rhiannon cried, falling to her knees. "Paul!" She tapped his cheeks.

"The dwarf—" I said, struggling to get my breath back. "It bit him. It bit into his side. Please tell me he's going to be all right."

I swallowed. My throat was raw and burned when I swallowed the lump in my throat.

"A dwarf bite can be vicious," the Three Ps said.

"Tell me he's going to be fine," I begged, but my words were met with only silence.

"He might be," Rhiannon said softly, "if we were near the Sanctuary. But out here—" She choked on a sob.

"Take him," I blurted before I could think about what I was saying. Because if I stopped to weigh the options, I might change my mind.

"Take him back with Horatia. Get them to the Sanctuary."

"That would cut our numbers and jeopardize the mission," she protested, but it was only a half-hearted argument at best.

She clung tightly to Paul's hands, and he held hers.

"What if I screw up?" she whispered.

"Rhiannon," I said, "Horatia's and Paul's lives are in jeopardy. They're more important than the mission."

She blinked like the proverbial deer in headlights.

"But Alberta," she started.

"We can come back another time to get her," I said. "You have to try, Rhiannon. You won't screw up. You care too much. Rhiannon, think of

Paul!"

Paul coughed, spitting up blood to add to the already soaked ground. She didn't need any more convincing.

"All right," she said. "I'll take him back to headquarters. Perhaps I can adminster some first aid there and then alacroport them to the Sanctuary."

Paul rolled over and tried to get up on his knees between coughs.

There was no time to watch them go. I had no doubt this ruckus would have alerted Gerrard to our presence, if the dwarf hadn't done so already.

The Three Ps were thinking the same thing. "Let's go," they said.

I followed the three elves, not knowing if I was happy to get this over with, or scared to death of the outcome. Probably both.

CHAPTER TWENTY-SIX

WHERE GETTING ONTO the property had been bloody murder, almost literally, getting into the house was proving to be easier. And that worried me. So far my experience in the magical world had taught me that anything worth getting into was highly guarded with spells and such. I supposed the dwarf was to guard the house, and since we'd taken care of him, the spells were dropped. The giant invisible bubble barrier was gone. Still, I couldn't help but fear we were missing something.

The Three Ps had decided to alter their identical appearance for me, so I could tell them apart and call for them singly by name. I have to say theirs was a much better plan than, "Hey you! No, not you. You! No! The other one!"

Phineas coloured his hair an auburn brown and freckled his skin. Pio kept his hair brown, but added blond highlights and a large mole on his right cheek. Philibert elongated his nose, even though it wasn't necessary for him to change a thing. When the other two pointed that out to him, he shrugged. He said he'd always wanted a longer, more distinguished nose. I thought maybe he just didn't want to be left out. I supposed if I was used to doing everything my brothers did, I wouldn't want to feel left out, either.

It was unusual at first to hear them speaking separately. It somehow made them seem smaller, a less formidable force than when united. I guessed that was to be expected, but it was eerie as hell.

Our goal was to rescue Gran and Savion. Given our current ranks and numbers, subduing Gerrard was only an after-thought.

I thought safety should maybe be our first priority and therefore subduing Gerrard should be our primary goal, but I was out voted. My plan was deemed too risky. Attacking Gerrard was unnecessary, I was told. Sneaking in and rescuing hostages was a lower risk plan. I didn't see how that was possible, but like I said, I was out voted.

We climbed the stairs and crossed the porch without so much as a creak. Who knew three tall elves in top hats could be so quiet?

We'd scouted for a window I could crawl through, but they were all the crank-handle kind and locked tightly from the inside. So we were going to do things the old fashioned way by picking the lock on the front door. I argued we should try the back door first, but again, I was overruled on account of the magic and the elves needing to be invited in and all that pomp and ceremony crap. It had to be the front door.

Pio picked the lock, and the door slid open. I slipped inside the dark room, shut the door and opened it again.

"You may come in," I whispered. I hoped it worked.

Philibert was the first to step inside. He did so without incident. That was all there was to it. The others followed, and we were all inside the foyer. Like I said, I should have known it was too easy.

As cold and modern as the house seemed on the outside, it was even more so on the inside. Where the Ottawa house was warm and flowery, this house was sterile and formal. The rooms were huge, the floor plan open. The main colours were black and mossy green. The materials were glass, marble and slate. It didn't exactly say "cottage", but it certainly said "home of the cold and calculating."

The only light came from green LEDs on appliances and an occasional dimly lit table lamp.

We had decided the hostages were most likely in the basement where I'd seen the most light.

The main staircase pierced the centre of the house with its black iron railings and wide ebony treads and no risers. And no where to hide. If we went down those stairs, Gerrard would see us coming.

Pio signalled me to follow him. We went in search of another staircase. We found the laundry room on the main floor next to the garage and the back door. There, we found the service stairs. We descended.

At the bottom, we found we were in a storage room, a pantry with shelves lined with canned food.

The storage room door stood open slightly, and through the crack we saw a short hallway with a couple of doors and one door directly opposite us, which was wide open and revealed the main room of the basement. A lab.

I couldn't see much through the crack, but I saw enough. A counter, and on the counter a microscope, and next to it, the blue orb containing Gran.

The top hat triplets saw the orb, too. We couldn't see Savion, but we could hear him.

"Father, we have to go back. I have to go to school."

"No, son. After today, you'll never have to go to school again. You shall have tutors."

On tiptoes, we inched down the hallway, keeping our backs pressed tightly to the walls.

"Father, please don't do this. I don't care about tutors or money."

"Savion! Enough, please. I'm trying to work."

"But the school will call—"

"Stop whining. I will take care of the school."

"At least let him go, Father. Don't do this to him—"

"Enough!"

Savion's babbling had provided us with good cover as we'd made our way into the house to the doorway of the lab. But he'd also provided us with new information.

I held up three fingers. There were three hostages. The triplets nodded in unison.

Three hostages, three elves, one soon-to-be-turner and one sorcerer.

I had an idea. I pointed my three fingers at them and then at the open doorway, then waggled my fingers like walking legs. And then I charged right through the doorway before they could make me change my mind.

It wouldn't have taken much.

"Savion!" I said. "There you are! I've been searching for you! You know the history project is due today, right? You haven't forgotten, have you?"

I paused for breath and was able to take in the room. For the most part, the place looked like the lab in science class: counters piled with machines like photocopiers but somehow I knew they weren't photocopiers but fancy machines that worked with blood; there were beakers, test tubes, containers, boxes of supplies, and reference books.

But science class didn't have someone strapped half-dead to a table, a student tied to a chair, or a mad man standing at the centre of it all.

"You," Gerrard said. He frowned, confused. "What are you doing here?"

I was all set to tell him again I was here to do homework with Savion, but when I saw the table, words failed me. I couldn't believe what I was seeing.

Only one word came to mind: "Rory?"

CHAPTER TWENTY-SEVEN

FEAR, AS ECHOED in Savion's widened eyes, took me by the shoulders and gave me a shake.

Merlin's hair. I had no idea what to do now. Rory wasn't supposed to be here.

"Uh—" I said intelligently.

Gerrard narrowed his eyes and took a step toward me. The air shifted. It became thick and sticky, and coated my skin in a film. I involuntarily took a step back, and then another until I backed up into the wall.

"Now's not a good time," Savion said, his voice almost a whisper.

"Uh, right." I swallowed. I couldn't seem to catch my breath. "Maybe I — I'll just go."

Fumbling with my hands, I felt the wall, searching for a way out. The fancy stairs were nearby. That was a good sign. I hoped.

"You are not going anywhere, blood turner," Gerrard said in a low voice.

I guessed it was safe to say he remembered me.

The air became thicker, sliding down my throat with each breath, coating my lungs, tasting like blood.

I coughed, but I couldn't clear it. I couldn't get enough air.

"I have to admit. I knew I would see you again," he said, "I did not realize it would be so soon. But do not think you are not welcome. You will fit into my plans most perfectly."

His smile made me feel like he hadn't eaten solid food in days and I was a giant slice of cake.

How did this happen? How did he get Rory? I turned to Savion for answers.

But the son of a sorcerer wouldn't look at me.

"Are you wondering about your boyfriend?" Gerrard asked. "I ran into him when I came home the other night. Found him peeking in through the windows."

I shook my head. "No. He went home."

Savion's eyes told me Rory hadn't left soon enough.

Dammit. Damn Rory for his jealousy. If he hadn't come by to check on me, he wouldn't be here. He wouldn't be in danger.

I would be able to think.

Right now all I could think about was Gran and Rory and how much I didn't want them to be here. What was I going to do? My part in this mission was only to open the door for the others. They were supposed to run in and save the day. Right. Distraction. That was it.

"Let them go," I said.

He laughed. "My experiment is having the best results ever."

"With Savion's blood?" I asked. "You're testing your experiments on Savion? Pulling the magic out of him?" Gerrard nodded, eager and proud. I gulped.

"Look at him," I continued. "He's too skinny. The experiment is using him up. He'll never make it to being a full spell-turner."

"Do you think that useless ploy will work on me? I've been using Savion's blood for years."

"Okay, but maybe Savion's blood isn't compatible with what you're doing. Perhaps you should try something different."

"What are you suggesting?"

"Use me instead," I said, before I could change my mind. "In a few days I'll be a blood turner. That's what you need, right?"

He examined me with a thoughtful expression. Thoughtful for a man with crazy eyes, anyway.

"Will you let them go?" I asked.

"To have you instead? That is the offer, is it not?" He seemed surprised, but pleased.

I nodded, unable to find my voice.

"To have you," he said. He smiled. "Most definitely. I always need more test subjects."

"Mel, no!" Savion said.

Dammit. I glared at Savion to shut up. No way did I want him screwing this up.

"Promise?" I asked Gerrard.

His smile turned dark and sinister. "Cross my heart and hope to die."

Oh boy. I was just full of great ideas today, wasn't I?

While we'd been talking, I'd been inching along toward the stairs. I backed into the first step, falling against the treads.

I had to get out of here. I didn't dare sneak a glance at the triplets. I wouldn't want Gerrard to follow my gaze. I knew they were there, by the service stairs, hovering in the shadows. I wanted them to get the hostages. I had to make this distraction work.

Gerrard stalked closer, still moving slowly, but itching to get his hands on me. He reached out, and that's when I struck out and kicked him in the groin.

He groaned and doubled over. His hands went to protect himself, instead of grabbing for me.

I used the moment to haul my butt up the stairs.

He shouted and stumbled behind me.

I ran through the main floor. The air was clearer up here, easier to breathe, but it was dark. I bumped into furniture, and ploughed into walls. Gerrard had the advantage over me. He knew his way around his own house.

I had to keep him away from the service stairs and the basement. The Three Ps needed time to alacroport the hostages out. Gran . . . God, I wanted to see Gran again.

I circled around the living room, and stopped to listen. I heard him reach the main floor, but from there, where did he go?

The house was silent. I couldn't even hear the hum of the refrigerator or the soft hush that the propane fireplace should have been making.

I hoped it was a spell worked by the elves. Maybe they were doing something to hide the sound of their exodus. I sure as hell hoped the silence was because of a spell worked by Gerrard.

My heartbeat was unnaturally loud in all that silence. Every breath I took was like a scream.

In that moment I became more terrified than ever before. What was I doing? How completely stupid was this? I couldn't face him alone. What was I thinking?

But here I was. Alone with a known, wanted murderer.

The unfairness of it struck me in the gut. Was my life not bad enough? Was losing both my parents before my sixteenth birthday not tragic enough? Was I too destined for an early grave?

Could life be this unfair?

No. I wouldn't let Gerrard get away with this. I couldn't. It wasn't right. There had to be justice. There just had to be.

If there was a way out of this situation, I had to find it.

That was it. That was what I needed. A way out. If I could lead Gerrard out of here— what? Lead him straight into the elves' rescue? Or how about right over to the injured turners? I didn't know if Paul and Rhiannon were still outside or not.

No good, Mel. Think. I had to keep him trapped here, but out of the way. So where to go?

I didn't think it would take too long for the triplets to make the rescue and get back to help me. I just had to hold on until then.

I needed to buy some time. I could do that, right?

And then what? Alacroport out of here? Yeah, right. And fail another spell?

Before I could think about it any more, I darted around the living room doorway to the front hall and hit the main staircase running.

From the moment I first laid eyes on that modern staircase I knew it would be a problem. Open steps like that? Yeah, that kind of staircase could lead to all sorts of injuries. One slip and you could end up falling through the stairs and down two stories. That would be bad.

But what was waiting for me was worse.

On the other side of those stairs was the very modern kitchen. Suspended in mid-air were all the kitchen knives. Evenly dispersed. Sharp, pointed ends aimed at me.

"You don't have to fight me, you know," Gerrard said. "You could live very well in my house. You and Savion seem to get along." He heaved a sigh. "I can't tell you what a disappointment it's been to learn he's going to be a white turner. He's useless to me. Always will be. But his mother loved him, so for her, I let him live."

"Savion cares about me," I whispered. He'd notably left out anything about letting Gran and Rory live.

"Ah, yes. He does. But that poses no problem. He does as his father tells him. Savion is mine. I control him. His care for you will exist only for as long as I allow it."

So there was my life laid out before me: he would take me, use me, and torture me with friendship. He would dangle Savion, the one friend he would allow, like a carrot, and then take him away, hurting us both.

My mother and Gran always said friends could be used against me, or I against them, and now I finally understood what they meant.

I couldn't allow it.

"Over my dead body," I said.

As soon as my foot hit the first step, all those sharp points came flying straight at me.

CHAPTER TWENTY-EIGHT

PAIN, I'VE NOTICED, is a funny thing. Why is it that I can slice the tip of my finger with a knife while chopping herbs for Gran's spells and not notice a thing until I see the blood, but a mere paper cut can hurt in the worst way? Does being aware of the injury make it hurt worse? If so, does that mean pain can be caused by a mere thought?

I lunged for a stair near the top, and hauled myself up, scraping against the sharp edges of the treads. That hurt.

My toe found a stair and I lunged again rolling onto the second floor hallway. For some reason, my right leg was sluggish and unresponsive to my request to jump.

Then I saw why.

Most of the knives had tried to follow me, but when I slid up, they ended up embedded in the undersides of the stair treads.

Though I hadn't felt it, one of the knives had embedded itself into my right thigh.

I didn't have time to stop and think about it. Gerrard was moving again. Thunderous footsteps raced toward the stairs. I yanked the knife out and threw it aside. Then I rolled over and half-dragged myself into the nearest bedroom and slammed the door shut.

I wanted to stop to catch my breath, but there was no time. I could hear him running up the stairs.

I had to keep moving. But I was bleeding, beaten, and out of breath. I just didn't have anything left in me.

I pulled a pillow off the bed and yanked it out of the case so I could tie the fabric around my leg. I'd just got the cotton wrapped around my thigh when   Gerrard burst through the door.

If evil had a face, his was it. The energy bomb back in Ottawa had taken its toll on him. He was physically weak and low on power. His show downstairs would have depleted what little stores he had left. His cheeks were sunken. The bones of his face pushed sharply against his pale skin. Dark rings circled his blood shot eyes.

"Looks like you could use a nap," I said, panting. "Been working overtime on your pet project?"

I had a plan. I just needed him to get closer.

"I have you now," Gerrard said. It sounded so corny. Like something a villain would say in a stupid sci-fi movie.

I smiled, and it started an avalanche of emotion. My shoulders shook with laughter. The laughter bubbled out of my mouth even as I tried to prevent its escape.

Gerrard frowned. "Something funny?"

Unable to stop laughing long enough to answer, I shrugged and shook my head.

Something told me he wouldn't get it anyway.

He narrowed his eyes. "I asked you if something was funny, little girl. You're about to die, what is funny about that?"

I directed my laughs into coughs. "Nothing," I said, "sir."

My voice came out in a squeal. He actually thought I cared whether I lived or died. That was the funniest thing of all. I laughed and laughed. My cheeks and sides ached from the laughter, but I couldn't stop.

It was all the distraction I needed. I reached out and grabbed Gerrard's leg. Then I turned the alacroport spell.

***

This time when the alacroport spell moved through my fingers, I thought about Ethelwulf. I thought about his apartment in the Sanctuary. I conjured his place in my mind, right down the weird things in the jars, the bits of straw on the floor and the smell of goat.

This time I worked the spell slowly. As before, the atoms snapped apart easily. They drifted on a beam of magic from the house by the Madawaska river into the place that didn't exist. I concentrated on slowly putting the atoms back together— his and mine, keeping the two streams separate. I felt like a toddler stacking wooden blocks. The spell seemed to take forever to turn.

We did not end up where I expected.

What should have been a crack and thunder boom as the last atom fell into place was a soft fizzle that fell dead in the surrounding mist.

Tiny rocks dug into my legs where the bedroom floor had been replaced with a gravel strewn path. A breeze blew past, sighing in the trees above our heads. I fell back and hit my head on the cement slab behind me.

Gerrard stumbled from the motion of the transport. He let out a growl of frustration. The air briefly tingled with static electricity. Then he hit me with it.

Guess he had something left in the tank after all.

He was ready to kill me. Pain and agony screamed from my chest and spread out, biting at my fingers and toes. This was nothing like fighting the dwarf. This was so much worse. My limbs twitched, and then my body rocked in convulsions for what seemed like forever. The power drained from his fingers, and I was left gasping, rolling on the ground, trying to make my body forget the pain. The air was thick and sticky and I thought I would go mad before I got a satisfying lungful.

I'd pushed him too far.

Clearly Gerrard had managed to control his anger and hide his power. It took the Council this long to even get close to him. Of course he could hold out longer than me. What had I been thinking? If I had enough energy to speak, I might have been able to taunt him into killing me outright.

And now that I'd brilliantly alacroported us to the Sanctuary's cemetary, the Three Ps would never find me.

I was doomed.

There was no way out. I wasn't a spell-turner yet. I had no way to open the cemetery gates, even if I could get there before Gerrard. And I was without the ability to turn a summoning spell to call for help.

Dammit. This was why I didn't want to use magic anymore. It was too dangerous. Anything could go wrong.

Anything and everything.

Gerrard finally released me from the electricity, and I understood what he'd done: he'd zapped power right out of me. I wouldn't be able to alacroport even if I wanted to. I didn't want to. Not after I'd screwed up. Again. But now transporting myself out of here wasn't even an option.

The removal of my powers left me trembling, chilled, as if I had a fever. My teeth chattered and I longed to cuddle up in my bed.

But I was a long way from home.

And a long way from getting out of this mess.

Gerrard snaked out an arm and swept a finger through the sticky blood on my leg. He brought his dripping finger to his face, first sniffing my blood, and then his tongue darted out, tasting.

"Ah," he sighed. "Your mother didn't taste this good."

Oh, Merlin.

An uneasy feeling slithered up behind me as the mist grew closer, taller, and more humanoid in shape. Faces formed of light and shadow, then fell away as new faces rose out of the fog. I shrank away from the approaching mist, drawing my legs into my chest. I tried to slip under the cement table, but Gerrard grabbed me by my jacket and hauled me to my feet.

He narrowed his eyes. "What did you do?" He seemed to just notice the change to his environment. We weren't at the cottage anymore. I was fairly sure he must have noticed we were no longer indoors and that it wasn't winter. Guess he was too preoccupied to care until just now.

"Where are we?" he demanded. "What is this place?"

"We're in a graveyard," I replied.

He straightened up, breathing in the damp air. He didn't know what to make of it. I guessed he'd never been here before.

Maybe I could use that to my advantage.

"In the Sanctuary," I pointed out.

He paled. His face tensed with surprise, but his grip on my coat tightened. "What have you done?" he demanded.

Shapes rose up from the mist, flanking him on either side.

"It's a graveyard, as you can see," I continued. "For the magically dead."

He noticed the shapes forming around him in the surrounding mist. He tried not to show fear, but his Adam's apple bobbed when he swallowed and he began to tremble ever so slightly.

"You've killed people, haven't you?" I asked. "Turners. Lots of turners."

"Get me out of here," he said.

I shook my head. "I can't. You sucked the magic out of me."

What I wouldn't give to be able to turn Gran's summoning spell and call Ethelwulf right now. I should have tried harder.

"You lie!"

"You tore all spells, all magic out of me, remember? Why don't you turn it?"

I realized then that although he had sucked the alacroport spell out of me, he had no idea how to turn it. He'd never used it. Gran said only Council members were allowed to use the alacroport. She must have been right.

She'd been right about a lot of things.

Wait— maybe he didn't have the alacroport spell. It was Council powers, and the Council powers Ethelwulf gave me were contained in the locket hanging around my neck. Maybe I still had the Council powers.

Gerrard quickly went from panic to fear as he realized the shapes in the wandering mist of magic might recognize him. He twisted and turned his body in an attempt to avoid being touched by the mist. The cloudy air formed hands that reached for him, fingers that poked at him. He swiveled, but he was no athlete. There was no grace in his movements. No control. He was going to fall into the mist.

I realized I didn't want that to happen. As much as I hated Gerrard Lebrun for everything he'd done to me, to my family, I didn't want him to die in the mist. I wanted him caught by the Council, held before the Elders and sentenced to neutralization. That was how this was supposed to go. Until I'd screwed it up. Until I'd brought us here instead of staying at the cottage where the others could find us.

If I still had the remaining powers of the Council, then I might still have the power to put Gerrard into an orb. Ethelwulf did it to Gran. I knew it could be done. I just didn't know how.

The mist closed in around us. It had crept up behind me, sliding over the cement table, cutting off all escape routes.

Was my mother in there? Was she part of the mob in the mist? I wished I knew.

Gerrard had run out of room to move in our small circle of gravel. I had to do something.

I called forth the spell for the orb. At least, I hoped I called it forth. I imagined creating a glass orb around Gerrard; I pictured it so vividly, my fingers hurt for the wanting of it.

That's when Gerrard stumbled. As he fell back, his arms flailed wildly as if he could catch himself before he fell into the mists of wandering magic.

I didn't think about it. I just grabbed him. I don't know what made me do it, but I couldn't let him fall into the mists.

As for the order of events that happened next, I couldn't say exactly. I remembered only a few details. The spell turned out of my fingers. I fought hard to get that spell to build a glass orb around him. I fought for it harder than I had for the alacroport that got us here.

While I concentrated on the spell, Gerrard's arm hit the mist, sizzling as his body was swallowed by the cloud mob. He careened back several steps, and the rest of him hit the mist with the same sizzle as sulphur scented the air. The orb spell slammed closed. But it was too late.

The momentum from Gerrard's fall forced me to stumble forward. There was no way to stop. Nothing to catch me.

I too fell into the mist.

CHAPTER TWENTY-NINE

I WAS DEAD. I had to be.

I remembered Gerrard falling into the mist, and I remembered turning an orb spell. And I remembered falling in after him, and then everything went white.

The gravel path was gone. It had been replaced by white, solid white. There was no breeze, no sound of wind in the trees overhead. Nothing but white. But yet, there was nothing I could touch. I tried to run to the white edge, but never got closer. It was like being suspended in a white room and not being able to touch the walls or ceiling.

I was in the mist. The mist of wandering magic. So I did the very thing I'd longed to do since learning of the cemetery and its secrets: I called out for my mom.

My voice fell flat. I called out again, louder. The stuffy air deadened all sound, no matter how loud I called.

I wasn't sure what I'd expected to happen. I just knew I had to try, I had to at least attempt to speak to her, to hear her voice one last time.

I called and I waited. I called again and waited some more. The waiting periods became longer, and I became tired. At some point I laid down. I was bruised, scratched, beaten, exhausted. It was no surprise that sleep came quickly. Sleeping was easier than dealing with the fact that my mother wasn't coming.

I woke up when I heard someone calling my name. Something crashed, the sound hurting my ears, as though a thousand panes of glass all shattered at once. The next thing I knew, I was on the gravel path in the cemetery. Most distinctly not dead.

Familiar faces loomed over me.

A clear ball with black swirls, similar to a five-pin bowling ball, rolled on the ground and bounced off my leg.

Then everything went black.

I woke up sometime later in a warm bed, surrounded by white. I panicked. I swore I was back in the mist. I couldn't remember what happened there. I only had the oddest feeling I never wanted to go back.

"Hush, now. It's all right," said the soft voice of a familiar female.

"Where am I?" I asked with urgency. The need to know I wasn't in the mist anymore flooded through me and I tried to move out of the bed.

A hand pushed gently on my shoulder. The bed rails squeaked and moaned as I laid back down.

"You're in a sort of hospital for the magical," she said. The voice belonged to Rhiannon. She sat on the edge of my bed. Her hair was different. Still mostly blond, but she had a tuft of pink at her right temple.

"Why is everything white?" I asked. Seeing her had made the panic lessen, but it wasn't completely gone.

"It's the purest form of magic," she said, and then she got up and moved away. I had a feeling there was something she wasn't saying.

"Way to go, Mel," Paul said, his drowsy voice trying for cheer. "Taking him to the cemetery so he could face the ghosts of his past. Cool. How'd you know to do it?"

Paul was lying in an identical iron-railed bed next to me. On the other side of him, Horatia snored in a bed of her own. It really was some kind of hospital.

"I didn't," I admitted.

"You didn't? Then why'd you do it?" he asked.

"I was trying to get to Ethelwulf. I don't know how we ended up in the graveyard."

Paul laughed. "That old fox! I wonder how he knew to change up his wards like that."

It didn't matter to me how or why Ethelwulf knew the things he did. There was only one thing I wanted to know. And as delighted as I was to see Paul and Horatia would be okay, there was only one person in the world I wanted to see.

Rory.

***

The bar wasn't packed, but I had a feeling Jared's uncle would still take home a reasonable profit from the night. I sat in a booth with Gran and

Ethelwulf— yes, really. Gran and Ethelwulf. In a bar. With music.

Yeah, I couldn't believe it either. And I was sitting right there.

Rory was up on stage, his fingers flying over the bass, sounding great. I was pretty sure he played better than ever now.

"So exactly what memories did you take from him?" I asked Ethelwulf. I'd asked before, but I wanted to be sure.

"The memories of Gerrard and Savion," Ethelwulf replied. His hands were splayed out on the table. His finger tapped to the beat.

Gerrard was safely encased in the large orb at home on my dresser. The Council members all thought I'd created it. I remembered trying to make an orb, but I didn't see the completed product, so I didn't feel like it was mine at all. But I didn't know how to convince them I didn't do it. In the meantime, I was put in charge of looking after the black orb. Apparently, if you create it, you had to look after it.

The Council also thought it was a miracle I'd survived the mist by putting myself into an orb at the same time. I didn't know how to explain I didn't do that either. I'd never created one orb before that moment, how could I know to create two? I could barely hold myself together, let alone a double dose of the orb spell. I wondered if it had something to do with my mother. She was buried there. Her magic was in that mist. It was a plausible explanation, but sounded crazy, which was why I'd told no one. I'd rather live with the possibility, than be told otherwise.

"Do you want me to take the memories of you as well?" he asked. "If I don't, there is always the possibility those other memories might return."

Rory was my first boyfriend and I kind of didn't want to give that up. He'd made me feel like a normal girl. I also wasn't over his jealous streak, but I was pretty sure Savion had had something to do with that. I remembered Savion's smirk when Rory had showed up at his house all full of fear and jealousy. And then I remembered the guilt on Savion's face back in the basement of the cottage. That sorcerer boy and I were going to have a long talk very soon.

Ethelwulf frowned, waiting for my answer.

"Take them," I said. As much as I hated admitting it, I felt better for having said it. Rory's jealousy had become too much for me to handle. I wanted a normal relationship and this wasn't it. If it did turn out Savion had something to do with Rory's jealousy, I could always start over again with him. In the meantime, there was no chance of Rory remembering what happened to him if he didn't remember me.

"Are you sure?" Gran asked. "I know this boy was important to you."

"Thanks, Gran. I appreciate it, but I'm sure."

Gran would have to be okay with me seeing Rory or whoever I wanted. That was part of our new agreement. I was going to have friends and go out and live a semi-normal teenage life. I was also going to resume magic lessons. That was also part of our agreement.

"I want you to be happy, Melantha. I was away from you at a time when I thought you needed me most, only to come home to find you are a young woman capable of looking after yourself. I was wrong to keep you locked up all the time."

"You were right to protect me."

"I know how much you hate magic lessons, Melantha, and I—"

"Gran, the only one I want to learn magic from is you."

I still had a lot to learn about magic. But I was no longer afraid of it. Oh, hell. I was still afraid of it. If I wasn't careful, magic could turn against me. Especially my magic. Blood magic. It was frightening enough to know magic had chosen me. So I had to take lessons. I had to learn to control the spells. Because the alternative was the magic would control me, and I wasn't going to let that happen.

But there would also be driving lessons and birthday parties. And Gran would be there when I graduated. And she would be there for other stuff. Important stuff. Normal stuff and magical stuff.

Because anything less just wasn't fair.

Epilogue

Several months later, Gran and I stood on a hill that was covered in wild flowers, the summer sun at its solstice beaming down. We stood in the company of friends, which included triplets who'd decided they no longer wanted to look the same, a turner who'd almost been torn in half, an ogre with a wooden leg, and the crafty old elf who'd brought us all together. We wore our best and many varieties of clothing, and smiled brightly, while a boy who'd once been a cricket exchanged vows with a girl who'd once had pink hair. And so wed by choice, they lived happily ever after.

***

Melantha Caldwell series
CATCHING A SORCERER
HUNTING A DEMON
SAVING A SPELL TURNER - coming soon
Sign up for my newsletter so I can let you know as soon as it's available: *http://eepurl.com/Wi3mL*

***

Thank You

Thank you, dear reader, for picking up CATCHING A SORCERER and giving it a chance.

Many thanks to my family for putting up with days without clean laundry and meals that came out of a can or a box while I was writing.

Special thanks to my critique partners, Cindy Dockendorf, Sara Bowers, and Becky from *Becky's Barmy Book Blog*. I could not have done this without your keen eyes and honest criticism! You are the best CPs a girl could ask for!!

I need to give an extra big thanks to Cindy for encouraging me to give self-publishing a try. It was just the right kick in the pants.

***

About the Author

Sara Walker lives in cottage country in Ontario, Canada with her family. When not writing or reading, she plays the bass guitar in a virtual rock band. She can often be found between the stacks of her local library.

Visit Sara online and read her free stories and find out about more books. She would love to hear from you.

http://sarawalker.ca
http://www.facebook.com/SaraWalkerAuthor
http://twitter.com/walkersarac

*

Made in the USA
Columbia, SC
18 April 2017